NEUROTEC

NEUROTEC
and other tales
Marcus Bolt

VIA BOOKS · ENGLAND

A VIA BOOK

First published in
September 2011 by VIA Books
Second edition October 2012, VIA Books
Copyright © Marcus Bolt 2011/12

ISBN: 978-0-9535766-3-0

Cover and book design by Creative Concepts, Bristol
Cover Illustration: detail from original work by Marcus Bolt
Typeset in Palatino-Roman,
Caslon Italic and Gill Sans Light
Produced through www.lulu.com

VIA Books
England

For my wife, Rosalyn

CONTENTS

NEUROTEC

ACER HAD NO idea how long he'd been at the outpost, or even what system he was in. He sometimes had the feeling he was born here, other times he thought he remembered arriving, but from where? His long-term memory had decayed, anything before yesterday a black dead end. He was contented, though – and he enjoyed his work, looked forward to it every night.

His living pod was pleasing, too; warm and cosy, about twice his height in both directions, with plenty of headroom, low lighting and neutrally decorated. It had a sleeping pallet, some storage space and, most importantly, his control and communications console. And the sims brought his food, took away his dirty clothes and returned them clean.

Ah, the sims – the bane of his otherwise happy existence. There were two of them, both simulacrums; automatons built to resemble his own humanoid, biped species; but they were of low intelligence and they repulsed him with their skeletal thinness. One of them was a druj-sim, doing all the cleaning and food prep, the other a scav-sim, out scouring the small, dull planet for supplies during the day and responsible for keeping the complex secure and well-maintained. Beyond that, he had no idea what they did; he slept all day and worked all night. Just lately, though, they had begun to annoy him, answering back, making sarcastic comments, moralising...

He found merely grunting, refusing to interact was the best way of dealing with them. He was certain he wasn't being paranoid, but he'd begun to wonder if their programs had been tampered with – some kind of virus? Planted by the enemy to thwart his mission? He knew he'd have to do something about it, soon. Reprogramming? Deactivation? Maybe he should contact headquarters, download a manual…

'Yeah, later.' He got off his sleep pallet and peered out of the view port. It was dark – only one of the planet's moons visible; the one in geo-stationary orbit that cast an eerie orange light over the dark, blocky terrain. The other moon had not yet risen, or perhaps was occluded by the fast moving cloud cover that often brought freezing, torrential rain. This was not a hospitable planet.

The druj-sim had brought food last night, but Acer had ignored it during the intense work session, collapsing on his pallet as dawn broke. He shovelled the congealed mess down now, tasting nothing, and clicked on his control module.

'Duty calls…' His mission was to 'seek and destroy' using an array of drone fighters at his command. He could control and manipulate the drones from his base, selecting armaments, flying into the war zone and wreaking havoc on the so-called Liberation Army – insurgents fighting the Galactic Order of which he was proud to be a member. He rarely lost a drone, but the enemy was cunning and it felt personal when he made a mistake, or was surprised in an ambush.

Checking his tally on the monitor, he saw with pleasure that it had been a good day last night and, judging from the after-battle reports, his superiors were pleased. His kill rate was high, he had lost no drones and he sensed he was contributing well to the war effort and that victory was close. He was hoping for promotion to Combat Director – and a new posting perhaps, something well away from this dull little planet and his malfunctioning sims.

Galvanised by this gratifying thought, he swung into the command seat, flicked on an array of control switches, selected a drone of his own design, took on fuel and ammunition, launched and began a sweeping recce of the current battle front. Dropping down through the war-torn planet's dense atmosphere, he thought it seemed unusually quiet. He came in low, diving into a rift valley, cutting power and gliding, scanning all the while… A glint of sunlight on something metallic ahead… he pulled focus on the 360 degree cameras, immediately catching a movement at the entrance to a cave – a rebel stronghold, or a lone skirmisher perhaps?

Making sure his defences were up to strength (no knowing what ground-to-air weapons he was up against) he tapped in the coordinates of the cave entrance, armed his missiles and pulled up sharply and away as they homed in, erupting into orange fireballs and bringing down half the mountainside in their wake.

"Yesss!' he yelled aloud, punching the air.

Acer reached for a container lying on his console, thinking it was time for a Neuro. Neurotec, his drug of choice, made him sharper, intensified his kill lust, and nowadays he found it increasingly difficult to work without them.

'Fuck!' The container was empty. Yesterday must've been quite a night. But he knew he'd have to go out now, the sims were programmed not to supply narcotics in any form. 'Some kind of in-built moral imperative,' he spat.

Going out onto the planet's surface was not something he relished, and he rarely left his pod. Not only was it dangerous out there, with metallised predators that moved with surprising speed attempting to hunt you down, but there was also the chance of a disturbing encounter with one of the weird looking, strange-acting sims that infested the planet. And anyway it was such a palaver donning the padded survival suit just for the long trek to the nearest supply outpost. And now his sims had begun refusing him credits...

Opening the entrance port, he peered into the gloom of the complex and then tiptoed as best he could in the bulky suit along one of the walkways. He passed a half open podport and saw the sims slumped in front of their entertainment module; as usual, it was pumping out its incomprehensible pulses of noise and coloured light. He found the scav-sim's work suit and rummaged through its utility compartments, finding a fistful of credits, which he quickly stuffed inside his own suit and then sneaked out through the main portal's airlock.

It was pitch black outside, no moons shining, total cloud cover, and he shivered as he jogged through the driving rain, dodging between monolithic outcrops of rock, following the tracks made by the metallised beasts, keeping his eyes open for the approaching spotlights of a guard-sim patrol – the last thing he needed was to be idiotically questioned by a uniformed moron. He had dim, nightmarish memories of this happening before. 'Not good – a real downer...'

The Neurotec supplier – a rogue-sim called Deela, lived high up the side of a mountain in a pod colony inhabited by outmoded and scrapped simulacrums. By the time Acer was rapping on the entrance port he was breathing heavily with the unaccustomed exertion.

'Yeah?' came a synthesised voice over the intercom.

'It's Acer. Need Neuros.'

'Got credits?'

'Yeah, plenty.' The port clicked open.

Acer hated being there. The pod was filthy, the rogue-sim scary looking, prone to malfunctioning and unpredictably dangerous. One wrong word and the situation erupted into violence, if you hadn't got out in time...

'Got a new kind of Neuro,' Deela told Acer. 'Expensive, but goes straight to the spot; you wanna try?'

An hour later, after downing a large quantity of Neurotec in exchange for all the credits, Acer and Deela were lifetime buddies.

'My sims, man. They're driving me crazy, ordering me around, giving me lectures, stoppin' the credits an' all that crap,' Acer confided. 'And I think they've been got at – you know – by the enemy; a virus; to prevent me completing my mission…?'

'Stoppin' the credits?' Deela interrupted, snapping out of his Neuro trance. 'That's bad, man. No credits, no Neuros. You gotta re-educate them sims…'

'Any ideas?'

'Up to you, man. Kick 'em out, juice 'em. Do what you gotta do…'

'Yeah, think I'll just fry their circuits, wipe 'em clean…'

Back in his pod, Acer completed his preparations. He made sure the sims were in sleep mode, lying side by side on their shared maintenance pallet, and began attaching cuff terminals he'd made from old food containers, in turn wired into a high power energy outlet. Satisfied everything was in place, he clicked 'on' and watched fascinated as the sims twitched and writhed, wisps of smoke rising in the air…

* * *

A small crowd was gathered on the pavement running alongside a row of terraced houses, the scene bathed in the flashing blue lights of an ambulance and several police cars.

'What's going on?' an early morning commuter asked a bystanding neighbour.

'That weird junkie kid at number thirty-four. Seems like he completely lost it last night; tried to electrocute his parents in their sleep…'

2

ENLIGHTENMENT

IT ALL STARTED when God got bored.

Now, this may seem paradoxical, because God purportedly exists outside of time, whereas in our realm, boredom and the passing of time are inexorably linked.

But, despite – or, perhaps, because of – being the One, All-embracing, Omnipotent and Omniscient, Eternal and Infinite Entity, the Lord God Almighty, The Supreme Being, The Source Of All Life did experience tedium and decided to alleviate the feeling by creating 'the gods'.

These He conceived of as a race of self-determining spirit beings with sentience, desires, will and individual personalities. He made them in His own image, thereby allowing them independence and creativity with access to abundant energy, and then set them up in a realm operating on a coarser vibratory level than His own.

God then sat back and observed their interactions, their foibles, loves and squabbles, their comings and goings and creative efforts as though watching a never-ending soap opera.

And it amused God greatly that one of their favourite pastimes was 'playing God'. They did this by creating highly complex virtual reality games involving finite 'universes' made from a variety of simplistic particles and populated with virtual lesser beings, purportedly created in *their* own image. For fun, they added space and time and death, then gave their virtual creations a form of awareness as a running sick-joke. And God merely smiled indulgently…

* * *

'Welcome. I'm Moderator Dayos – this is your first game, I believe?'

'Yes, it is.'

'Right, just relax into your solo-self while I patch it in. There – what can you see?'

'An intensity – filled with patterns, spirals…'

'Good. That's the game-play platform created from low-level energy condensed as space and mass, in turn supporting an infinite variety of physical manifestations. Extraordinary what can be done with a few dozen particles.'

'Space, mass, physicality? I'm aware of the concepts, but have never come across them before...'

'Something you'll have to get used to in the game. Very different to the way we do things here. In the game you can no longer will it and be there, or wish for something and it manifests.'

'So, how does one function?'

'To achieve a goal, it's necessary to negotiate space from within a biophysical unit. You'll enter as a newborn and, as you grow, you'll have to master the required skills of whatever species you manifest as over a period of time.'

'Time?'

'Yes, a most odd phenomenon we didn't anticipate, but of course is integral to space and mass."

'More to it than I realised...'

'Yes, there is, but you won't be aware of the dimentional limitations in the game reality – everything will seem normal, because that's all you'll know.

'Now, first I'm going to send you in on a dummy run. This will give you an idea of how it all works and then you can ask questions before starting the game proper. I'll send you to a system on the outer edge of one of those spiral forms you see. A popular venue, with many game-players – but they don't know they are, of course. And like them, in keeping with the rules, you'll also experience total forgetfulness of this realm, except for a few trace memories, an echo to help you focus. Are you ready?'

'Yes.'

'Here we go... Oh, well done. That was fast and clean for a first-timer. Just give me a run down of what happened to you while I make some final checks and adjustments.'

'It was extraordinary. The physicality is so intricate, so finely wrought. How is that done?'

'With a few carefully crafted mathematical formulae – plus a lot of energy. So, what did you experience?'

'An individual life in a body with a gender... I was very disorient-ed at first, but as I grew, I got used to it. It was cold and hot... and I was hungry and tired most of the time – but strong. I was on a planet we called Earth... I was a serf, working the land for a Lord. Then I died – my body worn out – when I was about forty... Oh, sorry, that's forty orbits of the planet around its star...'

'Yes, I'm aware...'

'Of course, I was forgetting. But space-time is the oddest experience. And death... the fear of death permeates everything... Wasn't all bad, though. I enjoyed things like sex, ale, laughter and my children – and summer when I was young – I loved running and climbing, and having friends and fun... and chasing girls – but then, I was forced to labour for my living...'

'Did you have any memories of this existence at all?'

'None – and yet I had emotions and a yearning for something... better. A kind of inner homesickness. My mind was uneducated, though, so it was hard to think, especially with only rudimentary language. And, as I had little or no access to knowledge, there was only a crude, superstitious religion to guide me...'

'Good, good – all very normal. Now, I sense you're very ready to start playing.'

'Will it be like that again?'

'Perhaps... but this time you enter the real game randomly through a gender-pair conceiving. You could be the progeny of an emperor, or a pauper. From there, you could become a farmer, a scientist, a ne'er-do-well and so on – the varieties are literally infinite. You could be playing on any of a billion planets, in the support structure of any of the game's myriad sentient species. But wherever you start from, you're only on level one and have many levels to complete in order to finish the game.'

'I understand.'

'Now, you're aware that I can't pull you out of your session? That you're going solo and the whole point of the game is to find your own way out and back?'

'Yes, I've listened to a few who've played.'

'And you realise there are those stuck on one level, living out the same life over and over? And that we can do nothing for them?'

'Yes. I understand the risks.'

'Good. Any questions?'

'Each life is a game play?'

'Correct.'

'And they are cumulative, leading to higher and higher levels?'

'Indeed – assuming you learn your lessons well.'

'So how do you know you've finished all the levels? What happens?'

'Oh, you'll know, believe me – a kind of epiphany occurs. Everything suddenly falls into place and it hits you – it's all a game and you are, and always have been, one with existence. Then, at that moment, you revert back to your purely energetic selfhood and travel home unerringly – to a highly fêted welcome, I might add – and much kudos.'

'I look forward to that. But how do you get this required knowledge?'

'You have to build it from the clues we leave in the game. They appear to get harder to solve as you progress, but because you're allowed to retain understanding gained from previous game plays, albeit in cryptic form, they are always solvable – eventually – unless you're stuck, of course. It is quite amazing how the clues and the knowledge get misinterpreted within the game, then distorted into belief systems such as religions and a whole variety of "-isms". Dogma, in short, which can get players entrenched deeper and deeper. Basically, you must avoid certainty at all costs.'

'I see...'

'Not only that, but the quality of the lives you lead, in terms of bodily, emotional and mental health, and the nature of the deaths you undergo, will depend entirely on the use you make of this acquired knowledge during the game. You will experience joy and suffering, pain and pleasure – everything; but you must break free constantly, starting afresh each time. Letting go – that's the secret.'

'Aren't you giving the game away, somewhat?'

'Oh, don't worry! You won't take any of this information with you. You won't even remember this conversation...'

'Nothing at all?'

'No. After each life-end you'll feel disoriented, your essence floating in limbo, and that's when you start trying to pull all the clues together, until you're suddenly called into the next game-play, and you start all over again...'

'You've played, I assume?'

'Many times – my solo-self actually created the game. Presented the idea to the Overseers and they indulged me, granted the energy requirement. The game has become very popular; we call it "Enlightenment", which is a most apt name.'

'As in lightening a load, throwing off burdens?'

'Exactly so, but also in the sense of "seeing the light". Now, are you ready to begin?'

'Yes, I am.'

'Comfortable?'

'Thank you, Dayos.'

'Then off you go... Mmm... He must be stuck somewhere...'

3

ENIGMA

UNDER THE ARRAY of spotlights, The President of the World Parliament could only see the first rows of the audience, but knew two thousand of the world's most high-ranking, wealthiest and therefore most influential people were sitting in the auditorium, and that ten billion viewers were watching her live. She wondered again whether her sari was too colourful for the occasion, but decided MC-ing the event would be so good for her ratings, a fashion slip would have negligible effect.

The applause died down and she began her speech as the autocue rolled.

'Ladies and gentlemen of the world, today is a truly momentous occasion in the history of humankind. *(Applause.)* It is such a privilege and honour to be invited to ask Enigma the chosen question in my role as the representative of the ten billion inhabitants of our planet.' *(More applause.)*

'As you know, the Enigma project was set up by the World Parliament seven years ago in 2040. Enigma is basically a massive virtual computer – a Grid Cluster linking, via our satellite communications network, just about every single computerised device on the planet with the databases of the world's universities, libraries and scientific establishments. Enigma, therefore, has untold computing power with all recorded human knowledge at its disposal. But as you may be aware, Enigma is much greater than the sum of its parts. Now, with the help of Enigma, there is no limit to what we can achieve for the benefit of life on our planet, no problem we cannot solve. We foresee a new Golden Age...'

Yet more applause, laughter and whoops from the audience. The President paused, waiting for quiet.

'The launch project chosen is to question Enigma about the nature of our existence here on Earth. The panel elected to create the questions consisted of the leaders of all major religions and our most eminent philosophical thinkers, scientists and mathematicians. For seven years they pondered, knowing the questions to be asked had to be simple yet profound, while brooking no ambiguity, and would satisfy people of all faiths as well as those with none.

'Of the questions finally presented for voting, the vast majority of the Earth's population has chosen the one considered as representative of all peoples, regardless of belief.

'It is now my heartfelt honour to reveal the chosen question to be asked of Enigma and, in doing so, to begin one of the greatest adventures in the history of this planet...'

In a storm of flashlights and whirring cameras almost drowning out the rapturous applause, the President walked across the stage to Enigma's control terminal. She held aloft for the cameras the golden envelope she carried and then proceeded to open it, taking out the card, reading the question, nodding wisely and smiling hugely – the whole well-rehearsed and theatrical event magnified on a fifty-metre wide plasma screen towering over the stage, and beamed live to billions of televisual communications receivers worldwide.

A white-coated technician indicated where the President should sit and handed her a microphone. She cleared her throat and said, in a clear, practised voice, 'Enigma, are you ready for our question?'

'*Ready,*' Enigma responded with synthesised, yet perfectly modulated intonations.

'Enigma, here is the question the world's population has chosen: "Why are we here?"'

A twenty-second pause. The world held its breath. The onscreen lights (flashing only for effect) came to a stop. Enigma was ready.

'Do you have an answer for us, Enigma?' the President asked.

'*Yes.*'

'Can you tell us what that is?'

'*Throughout the universe,*' Enigma began, '*raw energy is stored in vats, such as your sun. This energy is radiated to orbiting planets in order to begin a process of refinement. In Earth's case, the refining process begins with your plant life as they turn the sun's energy into carbohydrates. Once the energy is transformed and stored, your herbivores consume it, thus refining it more.*

'*The Earth's human species then consumes both plants and herbivores, refining the energy further still into a rich, psychic brew, which you store in your body units until it is ready for consumption by a higher life form – one beyond your comprehension.*'

A gasp from the audience and a babble of noise.

'This isn't what happened at rehearsal,' a technician muttered to the President, a worried look on his face.

She held up and waved her hand, asking for quiet.

'What are you saying, Enigma...?'

'Simply that the universe is a farm. You, along with every other sentient species that has ever existed evolves to a pre-programmed schedule – in your case, over the last six million years. This program has been designed to culminate in precisely this kind of exercise, and at this precise moment in time. In other words, you are merely a food crop that has reached maturation. That has always been your sole purpose. And this is why you are here.'

'Now hold on...' the president stammered, as the audience stood, shouting, running towards the stage, panic struck.

'Enough!' Enigma announced, loud enough to stop people in their tracks.

'My new Masters tell me you are ripened to perfection, and order me to begin the harvest... the reaping process is both instantaneous and painless; after, you will remain in store, outside of space and time, until required...'

Across the world, ten billion husks slumped lifeless to the floor.

4

A TURBULENT PRIEST

THE ONE HUNDRED and tenth Archbishop of Canterbury was feeling troubled. Sucking on an antacid tablet, he closed the thick report lying on his desk, sighed loudly and sat back in his chair, swivelling round to stare out of the window overlooking Lambeth Palace Gardens.

'The oldest continuously cultivated garden in London,' he mused. Then, with a shake of his head forced his attention again to the matter in hand, turning back to his desk and reopening the folder.

'Tricky little problem,' he muttered to himself. Henry the Second's infamous remark "Will no-one rid me of this turbulent priest?" floated into his mind, to be quickly dismissed as an unworthy thought for a Christian – especially for the Primate of all England.

'Why the Archdeacons can't handle this is beyond me. Wish now I hadn't offered to have a chat with him. The buck stops here, I guess. May God give me guidance...'

He pressed the button on the intercom and when his secretary answered said, 'You can send Reverend Wilson in now.'

The Archbishop stood as the door was opened and a thin, bespectacled and very young looking, dog-collared vicar was ushered in, nervously flicking his long, fair hair back off his forehead.

The two men shook hands over the desk. The Archbishop, once a college Rugby Blue, felt as if he were towering over the slight, young man and he experienced again the uncomfortable sensation of being too large, too well fed for a Christian, as though he had inherited and consumed more than his fair share of the world's resources.

'Take a seat, Brian. You don't mind if I call you Brian?'

'Not at all, Your Grace.'

'Please – call me Nicholas. This is not an official enquiry per se – not yet.' He picked up the report again. 'Now, you understand why I've asked to see you?'

'Well, I believe some of the Bishops aren't too happy with a few of my sermons...'

'That's a bit of an understatement, Brian. According to this report, all of the Bishops, and the Archdeacons, are extremely disturbed by virtually all of your sermons...'

The Archbishop opened the report at a page marked with a day-glo pink Post-It note. 'Let me read you an example from a transcript of one of your recent sermons – "When God decided to create the universe, He had no raw materials. He couldn't pop down to B and Q like you or I can if we were going to build a garden fence. Neither could He order a bag of clay or painting materials from the internet as we do when we feel a bit creative. There was just God – nothing else; only He existed. So where did he get the stuff, the energy, the particles, the matter, the stardust, from which He created the universe and everything in it, including us? From Himself, of course!" Hmm! And so it goes on. Now, wouldn't you say that was somewhat pantheistic? Perhaps not quite "on message" as they say – the Christian message that is?'

'Well, I suppose you could think that, Your Grace, but…'

'Nicholas,' the Archbishop interrupted while, this time, selecting a page with a blue Post-It note attached. 'And another example, and I quote: "The Abrahamic religions believe that our Creator resides outside of and apart from His creation and rarely intervenes, whereas others believe the Creator is the universe and every particle within it; and some hold that there is no Creator as such, but that the universe just exists and always has done and always will. Now no one, not our scientists, certainly not our religious leaders, can tell us who is correct – and does it matter? Wouldn't it be better if we forgot our differences, dropped our limiting terminologies, especially that word "God", so that all mankind could celebrate together the one thing we do know, the one thing we can be certain of – Life with a capital L?" In purely Christian terms, Brian, that is profane, is it not?'

'Your Grace, er, Nicholas, I was under the impression that part of your remit was to provide strategic guidance to ecumenical endeavours and that an all-embracing Interfaith was key to modern Christianity…'

'Well, yes, there is some truth in that. But it's a case of softly, softly catchee monkey; the old guard are powerful still. At every Council meeting, I have to face those who accuse me of profanity, even blasphemy, asking if I've forgotten that Christianity is the One True Faith, and that in leaning towards and embracing what they term "pagan faiths" we are, as clerics, going against our Covenant with God. And if I point out that other faiths contain good people, doing many good and humane things worldwide, they retort with "this is not is not the same good as Christian good, which equates, or should equate, with God's Holy Goodness". And then they tell me that we should not be embarrassed by our separation from the mainstream. They genuinely believe that the Multifaith movement is merely Political Correctness gone mad and is the work of Satan, undermining the Church of God... So you see these things have to be sorted at the highest level first, not in the parishes. Far too upsetting for the flock...'

'Ah, I get you. Reminds me of the old joke...'

The Archbishop raised an eyebrow and the young Reverend took it as an invitation to continue. 'A priest and an Imam are having a cigarette outside after a stormy ecumenical meeting. One says to the other, "Well, at least we worship the same God." And the other replies, "Yes indeed, you in your way and we in His".'

The Archbishop suppressed a smile, and turned to a page with a blue Post-It. "Yes, quite. Most amusing. But how do you explain this: "We have all been brought up and coerced, I could say brainwashed, into thinking that God is "up there". Our churches have steeples pointing to the sky; our hymns and prayers are riddled with references to Almighty God being on high – "in he-av-en a-bove" we sing; and we read that Christ "ascended into heaven" and in our common language we constantly refer to all things holy as "up there" and the other place as being "down below". But we shouldn't be looking for God outside, up there in the sky... we should be looking for God within ourselves. That tiny spark of His pure energy that He places at the heart of all things, be that a stone, an insect, a bird, a plant, an animal or a human. Have you ever felt the suffering of a badly designed or constructed building? Picked up the agony of contaminated water? Empathised with the cruel and unnatural life of factory-farmed chickens? And what of the unspeakable horror of tortured and maimed sentient beings? Yes, we humans are given the gift of conscious awareness and when we suffer, we know we are suffering... But if we develop our awareness and live by the one thing Christ said that makes sense to me, "Do unto others as you would be done by", how could anyone harm, hurt, torture or kill another human "for Queen and country"?'

Brian begins to answer, but the Archbishop holds up his hand, 'And this: "We believe that our body dies and that moment, our soul leaves. But I believe the soul decides, or knows, the time to leave and then the body dies when it no longer houses a soul. Fatal accidents, apparently healthy people dropping dead in their tracks, suicides, natural or man-made disasters are examples of this...". This is quite New-Agey preposterous, you know... where do you get these ideas from?'

'The Angel tells me...'

'I'm sorry?'

'The Angel, when he visits me. Well, he's not really an angel in the Biblical sense. He's more an extraterrestrial, but, as you know, all the angels in religious mythology, all "the gods" of old, were ETs. Or so The Angel tells me.'

The Archbishop, brow deeply furrowed, stared at Brian. He suddenly felt completely out of his depth, thinking this was a case for the psychiatrists now, but how to handle it?

Brian noted his concern and added gaily, 'Would you like to meet him?'

'Meet him?'

'Yes, I can try to summon him now, if you like.'

'Well, erm, er, yes. If you would, er, could...' the Archbishop stammered in alarm, his finger hovering over the intercom button, telling himself, 'Humour him. Don't antagonise the man...'

Brian relaxed into his chair and closed his eyes. The seconds passed. The Archbishop rubbed his brow. The room began to fill with light, gradually at first, then finally becoming so bright, the Archbishop was forced to shield his eyes.

'You wish to consult with me?' the apparition floating in the corner of the room projected into both their minds.

A cold chill of fear ran through the Archbishop's body. He recalled his mother telling him, when he was six, that if the hairs on the back of your neck stand on end and you shiver, it means the Devil has just passed your way.

'This is my Leader,' Brian said, 'the Archbishop of Canterbury. Nicholas, meet The Angel.'

'Do not be afraid, Archbishop,' The Angel projected. 'I am not the Devil of your religious mythology. I come in peace and am here purely for the benefit of humankind.'

Questions began to rise in the Archbishop's mind, and as they formed, the Angel supplied the answers instantaneously. "No, not an angel, nor a devil, but an extraterrestrial in that I come from a different realm, one that normally vibrates at a higher frequency than yours. The reason I am here now is because it is time for your species' next evolutionary step and we wish to help you. Yes, this time through your religions, rather than your somewhat obdurate politicians. Yes, Brian was "chosen" because he possesses a simplicity and purity of mind, making him more contactable than most. Think of lightning striking the highest point. Indeed, there are many such on your planet, and this gradual, transformative process is beginning world-wide as we communicate.

You now believe you are hallucinating and desire proof – come, I will take you to our realm...'

'But my secretary...'

'We will be travelling outside of space and time. You will only be away for a micro-second of Earth time, despite the apparent length our journey. Do nothing, just relax into yourself and allow me to transport you...'

* * *

'Everything's so astoundingly beautiful,' the Archbishop almost wept. Travelling at what appeared to be enormous velocity, they were now leaving the Earth, its blue curvature shimmering against the blackness of space as it receded to a hemisphere, then a sphere.

'I know I'm out of my body, yet I can still feel its form, still have feelings of euphoria, but no fear... and no pain! And no rheumatism – even my indigestion has gone...'

'Yeah Great, isn't it,' Brian said. 'Apparently, something similar happens when you die – but then we go beyond even The Angel's realm.'

'How can we do this?' the Archbishop thought.

'We're getting a bit of a boost from The Angel. We couldn't do it on our own – not yet. Not until our awareness has reached a certain level – or so I'm told,' Brian's thought returned.

They travelled on, through the length of the spiral arm that is home to the Earth, then across the galaxy towards the hub. As they neared the central black hole, they observed the event horizon, light and energy, inexorably drawn to the edge, tumbling over and down like a giant waterfall.

'You will feel disoriented for a moment as we negotiate the worm hole through into our realm,' The Angel warned.

'Now I truly understand the word ineffable,' the Archbishop mentally anguished. 'I'm seeing forms and colours never seen on Earth, sounds and sensory perceptions outside of my normal range. And the feeling, the overwhelming sense of goodness, of love! Just for a moment there, I recognised something I experienced when a young man, when I first felt my calling... yes! I remember now... How sad that the cares of high office have occluded that. I've been merely going through the motions for decades...'

'This is as far as you can possibly go now,' Angel projected. 'The short time you spend here will allow you to absorb much knowledge.

24

Knowledge and understanding that will be accessible to your thinking mind on your return, albeit only in terms of your human-ness. Use the information well... dissemination is key to not only your evolution, but to your very survival as a species.'

'Have you also...'

'Yes, we survived and evolved – in fact we are evolving still. Our history has been similar to your own in that we too started out as biological entities. Part of our remit, and essential for our growth, is to assist evolving bio-masses as best we can, just as we were once helped and guided – and still are. Your prophets, your scientists, and artists were all informed by us. We have been constantly monitoring you for millennia, feeding data to those who have developed the ability to receive the information energy. Yes – through dreams, epiphanies, trances and eureka moments. Your Abraham and Moses, Jesus and Mohammad, The Buddha and Confucius... and countless others; Leonardo and Michelangelo, Newton, Darwin and Pasteur, Picasso and Rodin, Bach and Stravinsky, Joyce and Laurence were all inspired by us originally, but they then interpreted what they were given through their individual human minds, feelings, cultural background and chosen discipline.

"You mean they all came here, to this place?' the Archbishop enquired.

'No – you are among the first; part of our new strategy to kick-start you into action. Time is running out for your kind, we feel, and we are duty bound to help – but there are no guarantees. We've lost whole species before, whole planets even. There always comes a tipping point and you are fast approaching yours. Even with your noblest, your so-called prophets, there was risk. We perhaps give them too much. They reshaped your society, but when they died, the living energy and knowledge we supplied became ossified – written down in your so-called Holy Books, where the message becomes a dead thing – merely a set of hard and fast rules, no longer an inspiration. Surely, you as a world church leader can understand that? Have you not observed how different your religion has become compared to the simple message of your prophet Jesus? Love your enemy as yourself, and do unto others as you would be done by, you preach – yet there has not been a day on your planet for millennia when there has been no armed conflict – usually blessed by your religious leaders. And your greed – even with your current, somewhat low-level, technology you could satisfactorily feed and house every one of your eight billion inhabitants... yet you turn a blind eye to tyrants and dictators, tycoons and magnates, all of whom hoard wealth for themselves, while your only motivation to act is when your lust for energy is threatened…

'Now I sense you are wondering when you will see God. You never will, and yet you do all the time. He is The Source of Life , your very being, your awareness. He is the motion of the planets and galaxies; He is all particles and atoms, molecules and chemical reactions. He is plant growth and storms and floods, and sunshine and wind. He is you and me. He is everything – the Great All That Is. You can no more see God or comprehend Him than a single brain cell can see or comprehend your own mind. And can your mind comprehend even itself? Now, do you have any more questions for me?'

'Well, something that's always puzzled me, silly really…'

'Ah, yes. Where does your soul go while you are asleep? In your culture, you have a saying that 'Sleep is Death's little brother'. This is a misunderstanding. Sleep is merely a lowered state of consciousness – as is proven by a mother deep in sleep, who yet hears and responds to the faintest cry of her newborn child. Secondly, consciousness is a function, a tool, a sense like vision or hearing. Humans, like all creatures, are many layered; so your mind, feelings, passions or soul can use the consciousness tool at any time. When your mind relinquishes its full hold on consciousness when you sleep, your soul temporarily takes it over, making use of it in a way your mind could never grasp. So, when you awake and your mind claims it back, you have no memory trace, no recall, of what your soul has done during your sleep period. Another complication for you is that the soul operates outside of time, which itself is yet another function, only experienced by the mind. I hope that answers your question…? Good.

'And now, gain knowledge. Ask questions, communicate with others and absorb your fill, for I shall return you to your own realm soon. You will only be able to retain faint memories of this journey and what has transpired; but we hope there will be a keener awareness blossoming inside, a new feeling of urgency and understanding, which you can use allied to your worldly influence. You are essentially a good man, Archbishop, but the burdens of office weigh you down – and be aware of your peccadillos, particularly your hunger for the trappings of power – it can override that which we have given you, if allowed, if you are careless.'

* * *

It was as though they had shut their eyes for a second.

'So, what do you think?' Brian asked.

'Well, I'm stunned. Something extraordinary seems to have taken place, but I'm having trouble remembering exactly what it was…'

'Yes, it's like that. But it comes back in dribs and drabs – during quiet or creative moments. But it's more noticeable in terms of one's thinking and feeling. Like there's been a subtle change, a clarity, something resolved…'

'Yes, I can see that. But it can be like searching for a word. You know it's there, you can feel its shape, and you know what it isn't, but you can't quite grasp what it is…

'Anyway, right now, what are we going to do about you and the Bishops, hmm? I suggest that, for the time being, we'd better suspend you, just for a while until we can sort something out. We'll tell your congregation that due to ill health, overwork or something along those lines, you've had to stand down, and we'll send a temporary replacement to look after your flock. And I'd like you to go into our retreat for a time, all expenses paid, of course. It'll do you good, very relaxing I'm told. Has it's own swimming pool, an eighteen-hole golf course on site and a remarkably well-stocked library. What do you say?'

'Well, I wouldn't mind, just for a while – haven't had a decent holiday for years. Stipend not that great…'

'Yes, quite.' The Archbishop had risen from his seat and was guiding Brian to the door, arm around his shoulder. 'I'll make all the arrangements and be in touch.'

In the reception area, the Archbishop shook Brian's hand. 'Goodbye, young man. You know your way out?'

'Yes I do. God be with you, your Grace and thank you. Exciting times ahead, I believe.'

As Brian disappeared down the stairs, the Archbishop turned to his secretary and said, 'Get me Archdeacon Smithson, would you?' and walked back to his office.

'How are you, Harry,' he asked into the mouthpiece. 'Good. Listen, I've had a word with our young friend – quite a disturbing experience. Not sure he's all there, to be honest. Anyway, I've temporarily suspended him, and he's agreed, so we'll need a replacement. And, meanwhile, I'll get him booked into the retreat for a few weeks, until we can get him assessed by our psychiatrist. We really can't have him spouting that New Age kind of stuff to his congregation, and if the media pick it up, it'll be a PR catastrophe. Could you make all the necessary arrangements? Yes, I'll send over a memo outlining my decision. Excellent. Now, I wonder if you could do me a small favour? Could you get in touch with all the Ecumenical Council Leaders – ask around and see if they've had any similar occurrences to this in their respective countries, and then let me know? Many thanks, old boy.

'And let's do lunch sometime soon. I'd like to discuss a budget for redecorating my rooms...'

5
THE MOON ROCK RUNES

DAVID ADAMSON, STAFF REPORTER WRITES (DRAFT)...

After a year of research trying to locate her whereabouts, and another of sending emails requesting an interview, I am at last sitting opposite the legendary Dr. Zhang Xiao, drinking green tea from an exquisite porcelain cup in her isolated farmhouse nestling in the heart of rural England.

The remarkable Dr. Zhang Xiao; *cum laude* graduate of Beijing University, scientist, astronaut and, after a sudden change of speciali- sation, a Nobel Laureate for her groundbreaking work on the now ubiquitous cure for cancer...

'Dr. Xiao, you're retired now, but you have had one of the most remarkable and varied careers on record. In fact you're considered a modern day Leonardo da Vinci,' I tell her.

She scoffs at the suggestion, but her smile tells me she is pleased.

'You were also the person who found the famous "Message in the Moon Rock", as the media called it some fifty years ago, back in 2062. I believe at the time, you were a hydro-geologist and heading up the first Lunar Settlement Program?'

'That's quite correct.'

'So, exactly how did you find it?'

The still alert and remarkably black-haired octogenarian laughs again. 'I didn't – it discovered me. I was collecting rock samples on the so-called Dark Side of the Moon when I caught sight of it – it seemed to roll directly into my torch beam, literally, and because it looked more regular, more spherical than normal and was glinting a lighter colour, it immediately grabbed my attention. It was about the size of a large grape. I was fascinated by it at once and just had to collect it.'

'And why did the media label it the "The Message in the Moon Rock"?'

'Apart from its catchy, sound-bite quality, you mean? Well, it's a lit- tle more complex than that. When we returned to Earth,' she continues, 'I and my team at Beijing University spent a lot of time attempting to analyse it, using every technique available to us – ultra sound, spec- troscopy, electron microscope, particle accelerator and so on. But its

29

chemical and atomic make-up eluded us – it was simply a hitherto unknown substance, somewhere between organic and inorganic I liked to think. Then one day, we noticed an interference pattern in the sub-atomic particle data. This manifest disturbance in the electron clouds appeared in data printouts as a series of punctilios. On closer examination, we observed distinctive patterns created by the re-arrangement and position-fixing of particles. We were totally convinced that we were observing culturally translatable replicators...'

'I'm sorry?'

'A form of language – albeit highly encrypted. That's when we began to hypothesise that perhaps the atomic structure within the rock could have been used as a kind of sophisticated 'memory store', and if so, what was stored therein, what kind of super-advanced technology could have achieved this miraculous thing, and who or what employed it? Unfortunately, the information was leaked and the press had a field day of 'little green men' type speculation.'

'You then headed up an international team set up to decipher the code, I believe?'

'I did. They were very exciting times.'

'According to the books and papers I've read, and all the documentaries I've watched, you never managed to unpick the code, and people are still trying today, but there is still little progress. Why is that, do you think? What was so difficult?''

'Well, we discovered several repeating patterns, or 'phrases', and we hoped they might become the key for decoding and interpreting what we thought might be a text – a process reminiscent of the early nineteenth century cracking of the Egyptian hieroglyphs on the Rosetta Stone; but we didn't have the equivalent of the Ancient Greek and Demotic script inscribed alongside, as Champollion did, or any actual phonetic parallels such as living Coptic.

'Not only that, as we began to realise, the pattern structure was completely different from any of the world's 7,000-plus languages, as well as those of animals, mathematics, computing and so on, all of which are initially developed through a cerebral cortex. In a sense, we were in a different dimension, way out of our league.

'We used massive computer power on it – I believe some of the programs are still running today – but we were completely floored.'

'Were you disappointed?' I ask.

'Oh, totally devastated at the time. I really thought this would be, at last, the proof that intelligent life other than our own has existed, and perhaps does exist, somewhere in the Universe.'

'And is that why you gave up hydro-geology and moved into cancer research?' I ask.

'Good heavens, no! A failed or intransigent experiment always spurred me on in the past. No, I changed course for another reason completely.'

'That's what I really want to ask you about... You were at the pinnacle of your career – world renowned, a media star, lucrative consultancy jobs and University chairs on offer – yet you risked giving it all up to start at the bottom of a new discipline – why?'

'Because the Moon Rock told me to.'

'The Moon Rock...?'

Dr. Xiao chuckles gleefully at my confusion and adds, 'In fact, that's also why I granted you this interview – the Moon Rock told me to invite you.'

'Now I'm totally lost,' I tell her.

'I've never told the real story before, but now is obviously the time. You see, I don't have very long in this world and the Rock needs a new guardian. It simply tells me that you are the appropriate person – we've been researching you as well, you know...' the latter said with an impish grin, 'and following your career with great interest. We believe you have the right qualities.'

She holds up her hand as I begin to speak. 'Save your questions until you hear what I have to tell; meanwhile, would you like more tea?'

'No, thank you, I'm fine.' I sense at this moment, the light fading as the evening closes in, that somehow I am about to get the story of the century, and, not wanting to miss a thing, double-check my recorder.

'OK. I'm sitting comfortably and I'm all ears,' I tell her.

'Perhaps eight years after finding the Rock, I was working on the data late one night, going over results, brainstorming, asking myself what had I missed? Had I perhaps merely come across a fluke of nature? Had, for example, centuries of gamma rays bombarding the rock created the patterns by chance, just as the so-called 'sculptures' on Mars had been created by dust storms, high-speed winds and so on.

'I remember picking up the Rock and idly pressed it to my temple, asking out loud in frustration, "What *are* you?" Immediately, it began to throb with light, each spherical wave growing larger with every pulse, until this iridescent energy filled the lab I was working in. And then, in my mind, I saw them and understood what the Rock really was...'

A silence hangs between us. The room grows darker. I am transfixed.

'In scientific terms, the species who created it were eukaryotic, multicellular, spore-producing organisms; I guess the nearest Earth classification would be a form of fungi. Their whole history downloaded into my mind in an instant. They lived on the Moon a billion years ago and were an advanced civilisation with a technology way beyond anything we've even dreamed of. They did not have brains, as we understand them, of course, but they possessed powerful "minds", had individual personalities and were a sentient, creative and highly intelligent race. Their society was complex, highly organised and consisted of family groups of both male and female genders. It was also revealed to me that monogamous marriage, offspring and the home were as important to them as to us and that they were essentially loving and compassionate, as well as having a wide range of other emotions similar to, and recognisable by, humans – plus many that are completely outside of our register. But, like us, they were prone to life and relationship difficulties and, therefore, greed, competitiveness, crime and political skulduggery thrived amongst them.

'As I understand it now, their language was one of feeling, expressed through movement of their gills combined with surface colour shifting. The Rock did indeed act like any human digital data store, but with an extraordinary ability to communicate with organic life forms. Unfortunately, I was not given to understand how they were able to manipulate the atomic structure, so it's still a complete mystery, I'm afraid.

'Sadly, they are now extinct – at least on the Moon. From what I have gathered over the years, it seems that a catastrophic meteor strike stripped their atmosphere, but they were prepared and some got away – although how they did that, I still cannot comprehend. Their technology is so advanced compared to ours – our attempts to understand are analogous to a caveman trying to fathom how a contemporary palm top works.

'After this event, it became clear to me that the texts held in the Rock were not constructed in a language based on the position of particles, as such, but more to do with the energy holding them in that position. It could only be felt, not read, if you see what I mean. I doubt it could ever be deciphered as such.'

'I don't quite understand how you read, or rather felt, the texts. Can you enlighten me?'

'Well, you could say it happens as in a dream, but the user is wide-awake – so, it's more of an inner vision. Perhaps using an analogy with computer data packets might help. They're delivered with instructions telling the software how to treat and read the payload. It's as though the markers in the Rock packet momentarily reprogram the neural networks so the user can receive and understand the feelings. Does that help? No? Well, how about if I said it was similar to an intuition? Like feeling something's wrong, or right, then later finding out the feeling was spot on? As though one were guided from a higher threshold than normal consciousness? It almost sounds religious, I know, but perhaps religion is based upon such phenomena and, because we have lost touch with that intuitive sense, we dress it up as supernatural – something "out there". Am I making myself clear?'

'Yes, I have a kind of inkling of what you're saying… But, what was in the Rock?' I ask impatiently. 'What was its message?'

'Well, how can I put this? There is no message as such, but a different answer every time it is consulted.'

'Consulted? I don't…'

I must have looked extremely puzzled, because Dr. Xiao smiled and quickly added, 'Not too difficult a concept to grasp. Very similar to Norse divination runes, or the *I Ching*. Do you know the *I Ching* – the Chinese Book of Changes? Have you ever consulted it?'

'I'm aware of it, but no, not really. You'll have to explain.'

'It's an ancient Chinese oracle in text form, packed with wisdom and advice, presented as sixty-four chapters – or topics, each with a related hexagram. You can ask it a question on virtually any subject and it will respond with guidance, which of course then has to be interpreted and is, on the whole subjective – but quite a remarkable artefact. To consult it, you have to verbalise a question and then throw yarrow stalks, or three coins (using their heads and tails), to obtain the correct hexagram. The hexagram that manifests will divine, or lead you to, the appropriate answer in the text. The theory is, it relies on the conspiring of all cause and effect at the precise moment of casting the coins, or stalks – a moment which can never be repeated.'

'Like tea leaves?' I thought, but held my tongue.

'You should read the foreword to the Wilhelm translation, written by Jung in 1951. When he was first asked to write the foreword, Jung was most impressed when he tried it out and threw the hexagram Ting; a *ting* is a ritual cauldron for both containing and cooking food. The *I Ching* told him that the *ting* was upturned and the food was hidden, but it felt the time was right for it to be made available again. Jung interpreted this as the I Ching being the cauldron and the food was its "spiritual nourishment". He also wrote that consulting the I Ching was like talking to a venerable person.. But I digress. I actually have the Rock here...'

'But how, I thought it was in the International Space Agency's museum?'

'I had a replica made – on its own instructions, I hasten to add. It swore me to secrecy and asked that it not be made available to the world just yet. It is a very powerful tool and could be used disastrously as a manipulative weapon by a ruthless government...'

A sudden thought occurred to me, and I asked, 'Is that how you found the cure for cancer?'

'The information it gave certainly helped guide me and my team, yes. It was its gift...'

'But how could it impart such scientific and technical information through feeling?'

'If you remember, the man who discovered the double helix of DNA was in an LSD induced dream state at the time. He saw snakes chasing their tails and the idea formed from that visionary image. The Rock works in exactly the same way – but without the trance-like state. Would you like to try it?'

Attempting to conceal my excitement, I say I most definitely would. The Doctor rises and switches on a table lamp, opens her bureau, takes out and hands me the actual Moon Rock.

'Hold it to your temple and ask a question...'

* * *

I spiked the piece I was writing. 'Disappointing. Not quite our cup of tea,' I told my editor, then, as instructed by the Rock, handed in my notice.

Events, from then on, unfolded exactly as I had been told they would. Dr. Xiao died two weeks after my visit (apparently sitting in her easy chair, a smile on her face). Shortly after, her solicitors contacted me to confirm she had left the farm to me in her will.

I've retired now and I too live reclusively in the farmhouse doing what she did as a 'hobby' for the last twenty years – growing mushrooms. The rest of the time I write.

The mushrooms, the Moon Rock and I converse much of the time. When I can interpret and understand what they are telling me I am elated and fascinated. Unfortunately, I have no science or maths skills, but they help me with my literary career – supplying ideas and concepts galore.

Like Dr. Xiao, I have learned much of their history. I have gleaned that some of them managed to escape their doomed home, and that a few made it to Earth and live their own separate existence here – apparently, the largest organisms on our planet are fungi. They accept our farming and consumption as part of life – just as we accept natural or man-made disasters. On the whole, they are contented with their lot, and their lives today are centred on their art and culture. They've tried to explain it all to me, but I can make no sense of it, much to their amusement.

My task now is to look after the Moon Rock and not to go public until they, or rather we, are ready – our species is far to young to grasp its importance and value.

In return, it looks after me, supplying my needs through its guidance of my literary career – as my latest 'number one best seller' demonstrates.

6
CHILD'S PLAY

"You summoned me, Lord Almighty?"

"Ah, yes, so I did. Moses, isn't it?'

"That's correct, Omniscient One."

"Good – now I've got something important for you to take back to your tribe... namely, the rules. Now, there are ten altogether. First, I am the One and Only – the Absolute, The Almighty, and you worship Me and no one else – ever! Two; no copying things I've made and then thinking you're really clever. Three; no calling me names or being rude about me behind My back. Four; you have to have a special day when you only think about Me – all day. Five; you gotta be nice to Me at all times. I'm like your parents, see, and if you're nice, you might get treats. Six – I hope you're taking this down?"

"Yes, yes, Lord. I am, indeed – on tablets of stone..."

"Right. Six; no killing people – that's My job alone. Seven; no kissing and cuddling anyone not in your family. Eight; no stealing things, or borrowing and not bringing back. Nine; no telling tales – especially if they're not true. And ten; no wanting what other's have; you've got to be satisfied with what's yours. Okay? You got all that?"

"Yes, Lord, thank you. Thank you."

"Right. Now remember, if anyone doesn't do what they're told and then come and say sorry to Me personally, they're going on the naughty step for ever and ever, right?"

"Understood, Your Omnipotence."

"Now go tell everyone, if they don't get themselves organised and start enjoying My Creation, I'm going to get really cross and send down plagues and famines and stuff..."

* * *

Elim plugged his long-distance transporter into the power supply and projected to the entrance of his domicile. He felt tired and in need of an immediate energy ingress.

'I'm home,' he called, floating into the changing cubicle to have work attire removed and leisure wear molecularly sprayed over his lozenge-shaped frame.

As he oozed out, Mila, his mate, greeted him with an affectionate four-tentacle wrap and mind-guided a refreshment module over to within Elim's reach.

'Mmm! I needed that,' he communicated after ingesting several glowing capsules.

'Hard work period?' Mila asked, soothing his inner mind with gentle thought pulses.

'Twelve chronars of simultaneous systems analysis and meetings, followed by non-stop report creation and filing. My work-mind is sore and I feel totally depleted – on the verge of deflation.'

'Poor thing,'

'How was your time?'

'Oh, the usual – thought-ordering supplies, overseeing the roboservers and tidying around.'

'And how's little Gaud?'

'Sulking.'

'Why? What's happened now?'

'I had to reprimand him.'

'Again? He's becoming a little wild...'

'A little more serious, this time, I'm afraid. He somehow transported into your homelab and... well, you'd better come and have a look.'

They thought 'lab-dome' together and entered.

'What's the problem?'

'I'll show you.' She commanded, 'Display recent,' and with a gentle hum the dome lights dimmed and a glowing, multi-dimensional space appeared before them.

'My Gods! What is that?' Elim expleted.

'I know, I'm sorry. I just took my awareness off him for a moment and he slipped out of the nursery... How he got access is a total mystery.'

Elim float-toured round the glowing space and began pulsating a nervous luminescence.

'And he did this all on his own?'

'Yes. I'm afraid so.'

Elim pointed to an area of the glowing mass with his primary appendage and thought, 'Enhance.'

An intricate pattern of rotating pinpoints of light manifested.

'More.' The lights became spirals slowly revolving on their own axes, each moving gently away from the centre. 'Again. Keep going. Concentrate there,' Elim pointed.

As the focus homed in, the image of a six-armed spiral glowing pure white at the centre appeared. The spiral was made up of billions of light sources with irregular spaces between each.

'Move in tighter. Good grief!' Elim thought out loud, startling his mate.

'What is it?'

'This is quite incredible,' he communicated. 'Look at that.'

The lab had homed in on one yellowish light source with eight spheres of various sizes slowly circling around it at different speeds on a single plane.

'Pretty,' Mila offered. 'Like a complex, but very elegant dance.'

'Move in closer still – that one there.' Elim indicated a blue-ish sphere.'Oh, no! This gets worse.' His body glowed the purple of anguish.

On the surface Elim saw what he didn't want to see – teeming pseudo-life evolving before his visual sense organ. 'Extrapolate data,' he ordered.

Information downloaded into his mind; 'Particle based existence; one hundred basic building blocks; wide range of physical manifestations; twenty million pseudo-species evolved from refined organic matter, only one species with pseudo-sentient awareness.'

'Open file on that species and display.'

'Bipods with rudimentary brains and self-awareness created by six sense organs; language detected with ability to express a range of emotional responses; rudimentary problem-solving abilities; standard pseudo-life civilisations with exponential pseudo-technological development detected, inevitably leading to self-extinction…'

'Anything else?'

'Delusional cultures typically based on Creator myth.'

'Explain.'

'Eternal after-life existence in imaginary non-physical space predicted for individuals adhering to basic behavioural rules programmed by artefact creator, Gaud, who in return must be worshipped; eternal punishment predicted for those who do not abide.'

'Enough. This is even worse than I thought.'

'Why? What is it?' Mila asked.

'Don't you see? Gaud is developing a deity complex. The child has somehow created a pseudo-universe with himself as Lord Creator.'

Elim noticed there were similar spheres throughout the system. Some were already changing colour from blue-green to dull yellows and dirty greys as pseudo-life slowly extinguished itself in the miniature time frame. Fascinated now, despite his growing concerns, he observed central energy masses also changing colour, becoming dull red as they rapidly expanded, absorbed their orbiting spheres, then collapsing back into themselves, rhythmically pulsing energy. He realised this was happening over and over throughout the whole artefact, and the energy sources were being replenished from its centre and the process beginning over and again.

'Awful, fiendish! I'm truly shocked.'

'I know, I can see your colouration...'

'If the Council found out, they'd have him removed for social reprogramming. And I wouldn't blame them; the suffering these types create when mature is total anathema to us now, and creating pseudo-life has been banned for aeons. It's deemed cruel to raise expectations like that in a semi-sentient sub-species, especially when lab manufactured.'

'But he's so sweet normally...'

'Maybe so, but if the Council finds out we've allowed this to happen in our own domicile, not only will they remove him, but they'll fine us heavily – and I'll possibly lose my job...'

'What are we going to do, then?' Mila asked, turning worry-green.

'Well, first of all, keep a closer eye on our offspring in future – and maybe send him to a discreet therapist for subtle reprogramming. Next, never let him in here again – he's too clever by half. I'll have to change all the entry thought-codes as well. And from now on, we must guard our recalls about this incident very closely – no one must find out. And now there's one last thing to do...'

'What's that?'

'Close and secure-delete,' he ordered.

7
AN ESCHATOLOGY

THE COMET WAS so close now, it rose and set throughout Sol Up, virtually filling the whole sky.

In the ensuing hemispheric gloom, and with only a fraction of a Sol to pass before it struck, those still alive and capable began descending through the gas layers to the main temple complex.

Each knew from connection with the central database the stark details of how the comet would rip through the layered atmosphere until it collided with the gas giant's solid ice core. The impact would release enough energy to create a small star, but not one living creature on the planet would survive to monitor and record the event.

'Funny how we turn to our religion at times like this,' Xylon mused to his partner as they swam down through the layers.

'Would you rather stay and get narcotised?' Argol mused back.

'No, I want to face this, in the raw.'

'Are you afraid?'

'Look at my cilia – they're pulsing with fear – I'm terrified.'

'Yes, me too. I'm glad we're together, though.'

They slid in under the bubble of the temple dome, found spaces in the tiers, locked tentacles and prepared to join in the ancient, half-remembered litany – it had been so many Sols since either had visited the temple.

Floating and slowly rotating around the heavy-gas pyramid serving as the altar at the centre of the bubbledome and addressing the whole congregation, the High Arch Priest sang out the last lines of the penultimate prayer.

'We're just in time,' Xylon whispered.

'Or just about out of it,' Argol giggled, then burst into a fit of sobbing. Xylon pulled her body capsule tighter to his, enfolding her in his tentacles until they merged as one.

'Planet Mother, pray for us who have digressed from your nature…' the Arch Priest thought-vocalised in a priestly modality.

'Now and at the Sol of our cease-to-be,' the congregation responded in a wall of melodious thought-sound, the gas curtains hanging around the temple's periphery shimmering with the iridescent colours of emotion drawn from the gathered crowd.

A charged stillness hung in the air, until the Arch Priest sang out, 'Many aeons ago, at the time of the First Great Judgement, our Holy Progenitor offered mercy and gave our forefathers, in His wisdom, another chance. They were pre-warned and allowed to gather and store samples of their molecular structure for the continuance of our species after the Great Solidifying that befell them. Our great ancestors survived, therefore, and have continued to warn us through our Sacred Texts that if we strayed from the path of righteousness yet again, a new Greater Judgement would be visited upon us. But unlike before, our Holy Progenitor would, we were warned, not see fit to allow us a further chance. Now, that time is upon us. Our species, perverted by wickedness and in thrall to materiality, must now cease to exist. We, the faithful, are also to be annihilated and can only pray for mercy in the After Realm, as we surrender to Our Holy Progenitor's will.

'Now let us utter the final prayer,' the Priest sang out.

The congregation responded as one, relishing, and perhaps understanding for the first time, the underlying realities of the ancient wording.

'Our Progenitor,
Who resideth in the After-Realm,
Sacred is your name.
Thy Realm be evidenced,
Thy plan be accomplished,
On the Mother planet, as it is in the After Realm.
Give us this Sol-up our elemental sustenance,
And pardon our transgressions
As we excuse those who have transgressed against us.
Lead us not into exothermicity,
But protect us from solidity,
For Thine is the universe,
Its energy and wonderment,
Now and for all time.
So be it...'

The Arch Priest began the final blessing. 'Go in peace to your Progenitor's home in the After-Realm, and may you...'

His thought-voice segued to a hetrodyne shriek. The Xylon/Argol combine experienced a rushing, searing pressure, disconnecting bonds, stripping molecules of atoms until their entity ceased to exist...

The gas giant exploded, plasma radiating into space like a spherical halo.

* * *

'Wow! Didja see that one go?' the young god whooped, leaping up and punching the air. 'Bang in the centre! Who's the Destroyer of Worlds, now?'

'Pure luck,' his playmate retorted.

'Oh, yeah? How come I'm two-nil up then?'

'Early days yet. My turn… Watch this – an asteroid into the third planet in that system there…'

8

ALL THE WORLD'S A STAGE

I'M NOT A Muslim, but I'm doing the Ramadan fast this year. It turns out Ramadan is the name of a month in the Islamic calendar. The fast lasts for 30 days. The method is, to have a light meal called *saur* before sun up, then nothing, no food or drink from dawn at 4.30 am, throughout the day to sundown at six.

This is going to be interesting...

Ramadan – day 1

Night time now. That was probably one of the hardest things I've ever done. I couldn't even doze off, my mind going crazy, just teeming with thoughts, mostly nonsense. I'm told it gets easier...

I've decided to keep a diary. Might turn it into a book one day. 'Observing the Fast' has a ring for a title – double meaning; observing, or keeping the fast, as well as observing what happens to me.

This is the first time I have ever been involved in a religious fast. Although my parents claimed to be Christians, they never did Lent, or anything like that.

I'd better get down the back-story before my mind goes completely. So, where to start?

I suppose coming home earlier than planned from a business trip and catching my wife in bed with Amy, her best friend, could be called the beginning. Anyway, it was at that point that I decided to give it all up – the sham of a disintegrating marriage, ailing business, home (paid for), the West in general. I was sick of the rat race, of England, financial crises, government lies, rioting hoodies, traffic jams – the whole me-me-me scenario – you name it. Capitalism in all its rampant glory, I suppose.

After a caustic argument, we finally agreed; my wife would keep the house, the furniture, the cars and a third of our meagre savings – she had a new career as a beautician, so I knew she'd be OK financially – and we would separate.

Our three kids had finished Uni and were all fairly secure in their chosen careers, so I felt I had done my job and had nothing more to offer. And anyway, my wife didn't seem to mind too much, so – *finito*.

Then I got out a world atlas, riffled through, shut my eyes and put my finger down on... Java. So, I booked a passage and left with one suitcase and a shoulder bag. We didn't even say goodbye.

Ramadan – Day 2

I got through today, somehow – the thirst was the problem, especially in this heat. I've just had my evening meal, so I'll write some more before I get too sleepy.

For the last eighteen months, I've been holed up in a village in Central Java with less than a grand in the bank, which should easily last me until I can start claiming my UK pension in a month's time.

What am I doing here, you might ask. You'll probably laugh, but I want to find myself – and then to discover the secret of life, the universe and everything.

You might think I'm a bit old at nearly sixty-five, but, in a way, I'm picking up from where I left off after college. It was dabbling in LSD that made me aware that there was something else. I saw that there is a world beyond this life, or rather an existence outside of the mind – I experienced it with every acid trip I took – but despite trying TM, following the Maharishi and even going back to my religion for a while (that was a laugh), I could never grasp it again, never move to that place I'd experienced on hallucinogens. That place where I knew for certain I, my real self, was a spiritual being living in a body.

But then the weight of career, marriage, kids and mortgages made me lose my way.

Since arriving here, I've managed to learn Bahasa Indonesian and got pretty good – at least I can communicate. The locals kind of humoured me and let me work in the terraced rice-paddies with them – no pay, of course – and they pumped me about the West as much as I pumped them about their culture and lives. They're a lovely people, simple, quick to laugh and quick to anger too, and very, very superstitious.

They have an enviable life in one way and are content with mere sufficiency. But that's all I can learn from them. They're kids, really, and just aren't interested in the philosophical life at all, which is no surprise as they're all devout Muslims, but with layers of Animistic beliefs and rituals – lots of ancestor worship, for example. They tell me they have faith and that's all you need; that and surrender to the Will of Allah, so there's nothing to think about, and then they shrug bemusedly and walk away shaking their heads, muttering 'Crazy Ingris!'

So, I'm still searching. I'm happy, though, I'm getting used to the heat and the mosquitoes, have lost about three stone in weight, enjoy being a virtual vegetarian and am as thin as a rake and brown as a berry, as they cliché.

Ramadan – day 3
Yesterday was easier, but still gruelling. Nothing out of the ordinary to report, so back to the story.

At the weekends, I used to go into the nearest towns and ask around. I was looking for a teacher, or a guru – they call them Kiais here, spiritual masters. I wanted to know more about the *kejiwaan*, the spiritual path of the *jiwa*, or inner content, aka the soul.

A few days ago, I heard about Kiai Sisdik Saman, who's about 80 and lives near the summit of Mount Kendalisodo. He seemed to be highly venerated, so, at the crack dawn the next day, I set off to visit him and to ask if I could become his disciple.

Ramadan – day 4
It's late night now, and I'm writing this by a rather dim oil lamp.

That following day was quite amazing. For a start, I hadn't realised Mount Kendalisodo has a shrine. It's quite extraordinary, about a two-hour climb up through jungle at a thousand metres, and near the summit. The shrine consists of four stone terraces, each about twenty feet long and three feet high, set at forty-five degrees into the rock face, stepped like a pyramid. On the top terraces, accessible by a stone staircase there are altars, with oval 'seats' onto which the Gods or ancestor spirits can descend – all intricately and rather beautifully carved. The most interesting to me was an image depicting Bhima, a character from the Wayang legends, entering the ocean in search of ultimate truth – music to my ears. First, though, he enters the tiny form of Dewaruci – in reality representing his own, true self – so the moral is that ultimate truth can only be found within – through meditation, or so my guide said.

Then a very odd thing happened. I was wandering around on my own after I'd paid him and he'd set off home, when I was approached by an young man, unusually dressed in pure white.

"What are you doing here, brother?' he asked. I told him I was a seeker, looking for Kiai Sisdik Saman – no one I'd asked so far had even heard of him, including my guide, and I was beginning to feel a little deflated.

'Follow that path there,' he told me, 'and you'll come to his house.'

I looked to where he pointed and saw a rough track disappearing into the trees. I turned to thank him, but he had completely disappeared. I thought this was a little spooky and it gave me goose bumps, despite the heat, but I set off eagerly along the track.

I'd gone about a mile, seeming to walk on a level, clockwise around the summit, through dense jungle, when I came to a clearing, a small *kampung* with just three bamboo huts of differing size at the centre. Walking towards me was a smiling, wizened old man, wearing a faded traditional *batik* headdress, a *sarong* and a formal, very ancient looking, black jacket.

'Welcome, my son. I am Kai Sisdik Saman, and I have been expecting you,' he told me, which took me aback.

He ushered me into the larger of the huts, sat me down and offered me tea and rice cakes, which I gladly accepted. Then he asked me what I was looking for, and I explained to him the best I could about my search for ultimate truth. He seemed to understand, nodding and saying, 'Ja,' occasionally. And then I asked him bluntly if he would be my teacher. To my surprise, he agreed, but on one condition.

'Tomorrow is the first day of the Holy Month of Ramadan,' he told me. 'I will be your teacher, but you must fast with me for the whole month, dawn to dusk, as is the tradition.'

He also offered me the smaller hut to live in for the duration, in return for helping him run errands, keep the huts clean and the undergrowth at bay. So, I gladly accepted and moved in. I've a sleeping mat, a low table and an oil lamp plus my bag with my toilet gear and a change of clothes – and this is to be my world for the next month.

Ramadan – day 5

I'm finding it hard going. The food is no problem, apart from an aching gut mid-morning. It's the thirst that still gets me – and then the anger. It's like a hothouse in there; fury blooms at the slightest irritation, such as a persistent mosquito, or a root that will not be pulled.

'Giving in to your anger negates the fast,' is all Kiai Sisdik said when I brought this up. Something is beginning to happen – but I've no idea what.

Ramadan – day 6

Breaking the fast when the sun has gone down is such a pleasure (and I never realised before that's where we get the word 'breakfast' from). A cup of water and a few dates is the most glorious thing. And then in the evenings, after a meal of rice and vegetables, I sit and listen to Kiai Sisdik, his wonderful mellifluous voice, his stories, his explanations, his gentle advice... He has somehow taught me to 'go inside' when it's hot (well over forty C around noon, despite the altitude) and to bring my inner temperature up by one degree. I've no idea how I do it, but it works – my body actually feels cooler and I don't seem to mind the heat any more!

Ramadan – day 7, 8 and 9

No entries. I'm in a mindless state most of the time, and just too tired at the end of the day and so glad to get into bed. One thing I notice, I now no longer need my alarm clock. I wake at 3.30am on the dot every day.

Ramadan – day 10

Day ten, and it suddenly seems easier. Kiai Sisdik took me for a walk down to the local village. The women there were preparing the evening meal. 'Stand over the cooking pot,' he directed me. 'Now breathe in. Do you want the food?'

I realised I didn't, that I wanted to keep the feeling of fasting more than I wanted to eat, I told him.

'Then you are at last fasting correctly,' he said.

Ramadan – day 11

KS told me that the first ten days are training of the passions – an exercise in self-discipline. The next ten days are, apparently, where an inner shift begins, preparing for the last ten days when spiritual knowledge can be gained.

Ramadan – day 12/13/14 and 15

Nothing to report – except that this fasting state seems quite normal now. There's a sweetness to it, an inner coolness as though I'd smoked a menthol cigarette. I can't think, or do much beyond mundane, physical tasks.

I almost feel like a villager – up early, eat, work gently all day, then food and bed (but no sex!). And I feel so contented, without a care in the world. I came across a magenta flower this morning, and sat gazing at it for an hour, transported.

Shades of William Blake... "To see the world in a grain of sand and heaven in a wild flower/Hold infinity in the palm of your hand, and eternity in an hour..."

Ramadan – day 20

Haven't been able to write my diary. No interest whatsoever. I feel in a state of limbo, no feelings about anything. Apparently tonight, the twenty-first, is the start of the Nights of Power as they're called – one every odd-numbered evening from now till the end. We will stay up all night together – another test.

Ramadan – day 21

That was tough! The more I tried to stay awake, the harder it got, my head lolling and dropping every few seconds. Kiai Sisdik kept nudging me awake constantly. I don't know how he does it. He seems so old and frail, yet so strong and... contained. He's amazing. God, I'm tired. And we have to do it all again tomorrow night.

Ramadan – day 22

Well, that was easier. Apparently, the reason for staying up is to receive the Qodar – a gift of enlightenment from the universe. But it'll only be in relation to how well you've done the fast, Kiai Sisdik said.

I'm learning more about him... he's a Sufi and Sufism is the mystical branch of Islam. He told me he was a 'covert' Sufi, not the 'overt' sort, forming a group with disciples and writing books. Covert work consists of a subtle introduction of ideas to individuals though the telepathic transmission of *baraka* (some kind of beneficial, psychic power), but when I asked what he meant, he wouldn't say more beyond, 'Understanding, thought and matter are all one.'

He never married and told me he was chosen for this life when a child, given all he needed in the form of *baraka* by a wise old man who visited his parents' house, but, even so, for the rest of his life he had to work on himself through meditation and *prihatin*, Indonesian for self-imposed asceticism, in order to understand the knowledge.

'Life is a battle between the ego and the soul,' he told me, but would answer no further questions on the subject, just saying, 'Feel balance,' when questioned.

Ramadan – day 23/24 and 25

Again, things are getting easier. I now need little food and little sleep. Most of the time, I feel as though I'm in a trance. Thinking is fairly impossible, but after the evening meal, the food essences feel like a drug washing through my system and my mind fires up – feeling sharper and clearer than normal. I'm also beginning to feel how my mind, emotions, passions are of my body and not of myself, or rather my 'self', which somehow seems detached from my body all day – and all night when I don't sleep.

Ramadan – day 26

The twenty-seventh night tonight. Earlier, we got talking about Quantum Mechanics of all things. I don't know a lot, just stuff I've picked up from the media, but KS seemed very interested and rather well informed. I told him about an experiment I'd seen on TV, the one where they bombard a piece of dual-slitted metal with light particles and get three bands of light on the screen behind instead of the expected two. The theory is that particles can behave as waveforms as well, and can, somehow, be in two places at once.

I went on to tell him about what happened when detectors were set up to monitor the particles and how they went back to producing only two bands of light.

Kiai Sisdik chuckled and said, 'Your particles behave the way they do only outside of time. But the scientists measured in time,' neatly summing up Heisenberg's Uncertainty Principle.

He paused for a moment, then said, 'Mmm. It would appear the Creator chooses when and to whom secrets are revealed.'

Naturally, I wanted to know what he meant, but he just shook his head and said, 'Patience.'

Ramadan – day 27/28/29/30

It was the twenty-ninth night last night, and today is the last day of the fast. I've got to attempt to put down what I experienced, but it's beyond words, ineffable. I had, what could be called an epiphany. It must've been around 3am. We were sitting together, not talking, just very relaxed and quiet – when I began to experienced a vibrating energy, a kind of glowing light all around us. At first it seemed to emanate from Kiai Sisdik, and then from inside myself, from the centre of my chest. My mind seemed to cease working, and then I seemed to float above my body, above the *kampung* and up into the sky. I even saw the lights of villages and towns and eventually even Jakarta. I know this sounds crazy – but I seemed to be floating above the world – I could see oceans, continents and this beautiful blue haze over the curvature of the earth. I felt no surprise, no fear; in fact, I felt nothing but this blissful feeling and a certainty that everything was all right for ever and ever – and I experienced... unity, and love. They're the only words that fit.

And then, I was at the Mount Kendalisodo shrine, sitting on one of the stone seats, opposite, but sort of united with, or linked to, Kiai Sisdik and he communicated with me, but not in language, but in waves of pure, silken energy, seeming to descend from above, through him, to me.

'How can we be doing this?' I wondered in my mind.

'Because I have given you *baraka*.'

'Extraordinary…'

'No, such experiences are only a reflection of a raised state of consciousness. In themselves they are nothing. The inner guidance received is more important. Quieten yourself and pay attention…'

I can't remember much of what happened then, but at one point what seemed to be a huge ball of light descended from above us. A creature of light emerged from it, as though it were some form of celestial transport. He (she? it?) greeted me with a raised hand. Understanding flooded my mind, nothing like my usual linear, sequential thinking, but as a totality, which unfolded like a flower at sun up – a story told by a new voice in my head.

'The whole of creation is made from a single energy,' the voice said. 'It can manifest as form in an infinite number of ways – a planet, a diamond, a tree, a worm, a human. being. But how does it do this? What is its motivating force? All is within the mind of the Creator, who imagines everything, creates the whole and sustains each individual part, be that a man or a photon, a microbe or a continent, moving all, just as the Dalang manipulates the Wayang puppets in a spontaneous and constant creative round, improvising within the parameters laid down for each universal manifestation…'

'Like predestination?' I thought.

'To a degree, but far more complex. The essence of all religion is surrender – and this is because we can do nothing else. It appears we think, act, decide, succeed and fail. We believe we live out our lives just like a small child sitting in the front seat believes he is driving the coach… But in truth, our Creator's imagination forms the physical entities of existence; imagining each of us, our whole lives, what we do, how we act and interact, how we feel, how it unfolds, how it will end. Knowing this removes all dualism, all seeking; it is the ultimate truth.'

And then, I was suddenly my old self again, back in the hut, Kiai Sisdik sitting quietly opposite me.

* * *

The fast is over – and I feel wonderful.

This morning, I tried to explain all that had transpired last night to Kiai Sisdik in order to ask him what it meant.

He just smiled and said, 'It is your reality,' and then changed the subject.

'So, now you have your answers. Today is Idul Fitr – a celebration for the end of the fast; and you must ask forgiveness from those whom you have harmed, and forgive those who have harmed you – including yourself.

'Then you must leave tomorrow, return to your birth-country and just live your life.'

'Yes, surrender,' I thought.

'Surrender, indeed, for everything is just as it should be,' Kiai Sisdik said, with an out-of-character, almost conspiratorial, wink.

* * *

That all happened a lifetime ago, it seems. I've been living back in England now for about six years. I'm retired, surviving on my pension and a little consultancy work, and very, very contented – and I never wrote the book.

In my absence, all my offspring married, and I now have three delightful grandchildren, and because of them my ex-wife and I have become good friends – we enjoy baby-sitting together and finding exciting places to go and interesting things to do with the little terrors.

It's Friday night and I'm sitting here in my small flat, wondering what the Puppet Master has planned for me this weekend...

9

CYBORGASM

DMGUY WAS FEELING very pleased with herself – she'd just won her first Galactic Grand Prix and was stepping onto the podium, acknowledging the cheers from an ecstatic crowd when, annoyingly, the 'reality-call' button began flashing on her heads-up. She eye-clicked 'pause'.

'Warizzit?' she asked curtly.

'Yo, Dee Em. Jst klokda zignal.'

'Whazzort?'

'System sezza Mayday – ole kwest 4 ade?'

'Gotta fix?'

'Bout hunnerd-thou dex at 2-sixty. F go now, ETA prox firty jiffs.'

'Salvij?'

'Praps. Notta bigee, do.'

'Betta av looksee. Gizza flash wenwe rive.'

Salvager's robotic arms had pulled the capsule into the huge storage hold and the whole crew were online, observing it from their pods.

'Eye deers?' DM asked the crew.

'Lks gen ole-tek,' MedGuy offered. 'Sys says no rads or bio-nastiz – jst inert ly-form inside – Erf 3 compatbull T n P.'

'Provnanz?'

'Poss Olederf...'

'Lezzopenit, ven.' DMGuy eye-clicked a tab on her control desk and the hold's automats went into action, floating above the device, gently and expertly releasing the canopy, scanning and recording.

'Wo, ugli.'

'Lks kinda ole human.'

'Aye – male. Hairy n well-endowed; neanderthal; yuk. Betta way-kit...'

'Oo r u?' DMGuy asked the man, who was now sitting on the edge of the capsule, head bowed, rubbing his eyes. 'Ju sprach Erf?'

'Just a minute, please. I'm feeling very dizzy, nauseous...'

'Vitas,' DM ordered and an automat floated across with an array of liquid dispensers and pharmas on an oval platter... The man grabbed a flask and drank deep.

'Thanks. Feeling much better now.' He cleared his throat and said, 'I am Flight Lieutenant Roger Galsworthy, Medical and Scientific Officer on Zeus Four, Jupiter Moons mission.'

The crew giggled – sensing something peculiar about the man's language and voice tone.

'Where am I? Who am I talking to, please?'

'On *Scavinja* – we salvij vess outta Erf Free. Me Dee em Guy.'

'Sorry? Dee-em guy?'

'Deesiz Mayka Guy, Class 1 – temp.'

'And where exactly are we?'

'Loc8 in fird glactick spiral, nth secta – mor2poynt, wot u doin out eer, flotin' rahn in vat fing?'

'I don't know where "here" is. The last thing I remember was closing the hatch on this cryo-stasis unit minutes before take off.'

'Wendat?'

'The twentieth of December, 2031. What's the date now?'

There were audible hoots from the crew.

'First Kwarter, 2540 Erf Free,' DMGuy laughed.

* * *

Over the next hour, the crew, with the help of System, searched through old Earth 1 archives, contriving to piece together Roger's story. Sys had even managed to retrieve, decipher and upgrade archaic video footage of the Jupiter Moons mission launch. Its two dimensionality, poor colour and sound quality in combination with the oldtech on display leaving the crew highly amused.

Roger, meanwhile, had slowly regained bodily control, and was managing to walk around the hold unaided by automats. The crew had sent him a one-piece garment and vita-tubes, and he'd let the automats inject them, but he was still feeling nauseous and disoriented.

Sys could only surmise that Roger and the rest of the five man crew had been ejected in advance of some catastrophic event – a meteor strike, or propulsion drive failure. How he and the capsule had survived for over 500 Earth 1 years was a complete mystery, even to Sys, who could only offer that, as the capsule was maintained by oldtech solar panels and recycling equipment, he had been lucky; no malfunctions and always drifting close enough to various stars to pick up the requisite energy.

'Yude betta tak sum R n R, now – we tlk mo l8er. I get automat take u2 restpod.'

'How come I haven't seen any of you people yet?' Roger queried. 'Are you running some kind of quarantine program?'

'Nah,' DM replied. 'No do face2face ennimor. Infac, we not acshulli on ship...'

* * *

'Wot we gunnado wittim?' DM asked StratGuy on the closed-loop comms.

'Dunno, guy. Buv mi lev. Sys sez takeback 2 Erf 3 – handover 2 ForityGuys. Jeez, he weerd – freaksme. Nokan handul. Gotta gt bk 2 UvverWorld – C U,' and with that, StratGuy closed the link.

DMGuy understood how he felt. She too was uncomfortable with this reality event, but she was intrigued. She wanted to know more, but the only way she could even contemplate such intimate interaction with an old human, especially one from so far back, was to get their reality-find into OtherWorld...

'Roger, thanks to Sys, I can talk to you now in your vernacular... Can you see that headband lying on the table beside you? Yes, that's it – now could you slip it on?'

'Aagh!' Roger wailed, and immediately pulled the headband off. 'Jesus, what is that?' he shouted.

'Sorry. That's OtherWorld – how we interact now; you know – socialise.'

'I'm a trained astronaut, but I can't take that. Too disorienting.'

'You'll have to get used to it – it's only a multi-dimensional headsup display of a virtual world. I had the automats make the headband for you, but in time, you'll have to learn to do this for yourself, develop the necessary neural networks. All in the mind, anyway, whether it's so-called reality or a common, cybergenerated reality.'

'Oh, Christ! Do I really have to go through all this palaver?'

'If you want to relate to others, yes. Come on now. All these things existed in your day, although not as sophisticated and complex. I've just been checking it all out with Sys.'

Roger tried again, and slowly, over the next hour, DMGuy helped him to overcome and then stabilise his mental and emotional anti-reactions.

'Right. This is me,' DMGuy announced. 'In OtherWorld, I'm labelled Samphire.'

Into his cabin floated what seemed to his sensibilities a comic book character – a tall, large-breasted, dark green-skinned beauty, her nakedness half-covered by cascading magenta hair.

'I can't see you at the moment,' Samphire said, 'You're just a blurred shape. We're going to have to fit you up with an avatar – I believe that's the term used in your day – a symbolic projection of yourself, albeit highly personalised to express your unique EyeD.'

Roger groaned, closing his eyes and shaking his head in disbelief.

'Right, on the control panel floating on your left periphery, you'll see an "EyeD-create" button. I want you to look at it and blink – that's an eye-click nav. Now do the same with one of the formatters displayed. Good, now "dress". Excellent, I can see you now. You look kinda funny, but we'll refine you as we go. Might as well keep the label Roger, for now.'

'I don't really understand why all this is necessary,' Roger said. 'I mean, we all live in the real, physical world regardless, so why the charade?'

'Thought you might ask, so I've been doing some research. System says it's down to evolution – here, I'll patch in her response – too sci-tech for me.'

'Since the advent of personal computers in the latter quarter of the twentieth century,' Roger saw, read and heard all at the same time, 'screen-based digitised information, social connectivity and game-play interaction had as big an impact on the structuring of the human brain as the original creation of language in all its manifestations, spoken, written and printed.

'Consequently, the brain's facility for neurogenesis has forged new neuronal complexes, thus dramatically altering human minds. However, this capacity was only fully realised and accepted in late 2200 after a century of trans-humanisation, during which, the desire for the perfect body and face, created with gene manipulation, nano-medics and robotic plastic surgery, began to have adverse psychosomatic side-effects. Everybody looked identical and began behaving the same, causing serious mental trauma for individuals and extreme psychological destabilisation for society.

'In short, humans need a sense of individuality or their mental health suffers. There was no going back to the ancient ways of inter-relating, or reversing two centuries of gene manipulation – it was as unpalatable to the new generations as killing, skinning and gutting animals for food was to even 21st century Westerners.

'With the concurrent advancement of organic computer technology and automated living, humans tacitly created a super-real, virtual world in preference to the unreliable, and troublesome, "real" world of human socialising. Today, the twenty billion plus population of each of the three inhabited planets, Earth 1, 2 and 3, live out the whole their waking day in OtherWorld, leaving the automats to look after the mundane business of ordinary existence, the maintenance of essential services and the smooth running of civilisation, merely supervised by volunteer humans on a rota basis...'

'My God!' Roger interjected, attempting to locate Samphire. 'Do you mean you never meet in the real world, ever?'

'Never,' she answered. 'There are ten of us on this ship, and we've been out searching for salvage for about five Earth 1 years and could never meet physically – we only meet in OtherWorld, patched through to the ship. The ship runs itself, but occasionally someone has to override Sys, make decisions, change a set course and so on. That's my job this year, and why I'm called DMGuy. We only have temporary labels for OuterWorld roles.'

'So you've never held someone's hand, kissed, made love?'

'Sure – in OtherWorld. Computers can emulate every human sensation by stimulating the correct parts of the brain from eating, to dancing through to sex – here, let me show you. Hold out your hand.'

'My God! What was that?' Roger cried, recoiling from the virtual finger tip stroke.

'That was an erotic pass,' Samphire laughed. 'You're going to have to learn all about virtual sex. There's no physicality on Earth 3, and no one to do it with, anyway.'

'How the hell do you reproduce?' Roger asked.

'You people had IVF and cloning in your day, no? We do something similar, but it's all controlled and sorted by the Med and Politico Systems. They decide on population levels, while the automats handle cloning, birth and early growth.'

'Brave New World...'

'What?'

'Nothing. Never mind.'

'Having OtherWorld sex is one of our most popular pastimes and having as many cyborgasms with as many others as possible is considered very healthy for the mindself. But if anyone wants a 'family', they can have one in OtherWorld – as many virtual offspring as they like, as long as they can afford them. I believe some women even go virtual for the pain/pleasure experience of pregnancy and childbirth; but they're considered weirdos.'

'What did you mean by "afford them"?'

'There still ain't no free lunch, so you have to either work in OtherWorld, creating virtual wealth, or do a virtual job – astronaut, politico, or perhaps scientist, but indirectly connected with the so-called real world. Such roles give you credit in OtherWorld. I've earned a fortune on this run; I probably won't need to ever work again.

'We get a ten percent bonus on all the salvage as well – wonder what you're going to be worth? Lotta people will want a part of you.'

'So I'm to be some kind of goddam freak show, huh?'

'Well, what do you think?' Samphire laughed, 'We don't come across real old-time bodies in space every day. You could be a star, but they'll probably want to study you. Maybe they'll recreate your story as a virtual life, who knows? Get up to speed as fast as you can, will you? I think you and I could be good together in OtherWorld. And I'd love to be the first to have a full cyborgasm session with you...'

* * *

'Sys, can I talk to you?'

'Yes, Roger. How can I help?'

'Tell me honestly, what do you think of my chances of surviving on Earth 3?'

'You'll survive physically. Medicine and all aspects of health are totally controlled by virtually infallible Systems such as myself. The latest generations of humans will have life spans of over five hundred years – and, of course, you've survived that long already.

'But, you won't survive mentally, to be honest. I think it's only fair to tell you that you will never meet any other humans "face to face" as you call it. There are no faces any more. You'd be the only human walking on the planet, and would have to be under a kind of house arrest, constantly monitored – there's nowhere to go. From my research, I forecast it will be loneliness that will destroy your sanity.'

'But why? I don't get it...'

'Today's human is just a mindself existing in the support structure of a bodiless brain floating in amniotic fluid. They live in a virtual world, their minds stimulated cyborganically to experience everything the old mind and body did, but without the risks of personal, physical and biological interaction, including illness, pain – especially emotional pain – and death. If they don't like a scenario they've created, or if things get out of hand, they can just think "delete" and start over... And they are all housed in hives – racks and racks of them covering the three Earths.'

'So, they've become biological computers?'

'An interesting concept, but not quite accurate in that they have Systems like me to do the actual computing for them – and the day to day smooth running of the world – the living, in other words. They just enjoy themselves in what they call OtherWorld, where they can choose the perfect lifestyle, over and over again. And we're working together with them to dispense with even the brain carrier and then the brain itself. We are programmed to assist them to become pure mindself energy.

'Now, the question remains, is it possible for you to short circuit the last five hundred years of evolution? It may be physically feasible, but would your unevolved mind cope? To answer that, we'll have to hand you over to a specialist Neuro-Sys, who will assess you and make the decision. But I doubt you could be assimilated.'

'So, I couldn't live as I am, and to live on Earth 3, I'd have to undergo this transformation and assimilation process; and, on top of that, my mind might not be able to handle it. What happens to me if it can't?

'We don't know, of course. The question has never arisen before. You're quite unique. But, I guess it would make life very difficult for you. You'll probably go insane with no one or anything to help you...'

'Hmmm. System, could you do something for me me? Could you get the automats to put me back in my pod and launch me into space again?'

'I could, but you won't survive this time. The technology's too old; you'll freeze or fry...'

'To be honest, I don't care. I'd prefer death to a living hell...'

10

IN VINO VERITAS

'GABRIEL! GOOD TO see you.'

'You too, Michael. How are you?'

'Fine thanks. Good journey?'

'Very smooth. Almost instantaneous, portal to portal; hardly any traffic queuing around the worm holes.'

'Good. And how's the Old Man?'

'Omnipotent as ever. You should visit Him.'

'I know – but my estate needs all my attention.'

'Actually, He sent me. Wants to know what you're up to.'

"As if He didn't know... Can I get you some refreshment?'

'Thank you.'

'Here, try this. A Premier Cru, our own label – Ambrosia.'

'Mmm. Lovely nose. Oh, that's good. I'm getting anger, lust and acrimony – and a beautiful, delicate finish... what is that? Affection? A very fine wine. So, tell me how you do it...'

'Let's take a tour and I'll show you...'

'It's breathtaking. How big did you say?'

'About forty billion lightcubes with over 300 billion energy sources and at least five times that many growing units.'

'Impressive. And how often do you harvest? Is there a season?'

'I wish. Growing units mature randomly so it's a never ending process.'

'How do you actually turn it into wine though?'

'Come, there's a unit ready for harvesting on one of the spiral arms; I'll show you exactly what we do...'

'Whoa! This looks a mess to me.'

'Yes, not a pretty sight is it? This one was seeded about four billion years ago, and has evolved bang on target, with the fruit – its sentient beings – emerging only fairly recently. Always these last stages that are so fascinating.'

'Good grief! What just happened?'

'You caught that, did you? The inhabitants of all our units are pre-programmed with the ability to create exponential technological growth in parallel with moral decline. They can't handle it of course, which means they either blow the planter-unit sky-high with some kind of internecine warfare, pollute the environment so it can no longer support life, or just wear it out – one of those usually does the trick. The ruling species of this unit, for example, just wiped themselves out, all ten billion of them. They overstretched their resources through rampant greed and simply withered on the vine, so to speak. They're now being harvested.'

'And how do you do that?'

'Simple, really. Each individual fruit releases its vital content when its carrier ceases to function. This psychic energy flounders around, completely lost in an incorporeal realm it doesn't understand. So we just siphon it off into vats, where we store all the emotion and passion it experienced in its so-called "lifetime", which then ferments until ready. Follow me – I'll show you our storage facilities in our central black hole...'

'Phew! Not pleasant, is it? You can smell the raw fear – and that wailing! Horrible. And you say they are sentient, so are they aware what's happening to them?'

'Not *that* sentient! But with all species, no matter what their elemental make up, the cultures they create are always based on an immortality myth – usually some concept of paradise in store for those who adhere to a strict moral code they invent, or eternal damnation for those who don't – the saintly and the wicked, the saved and the damned in their terms. And that wide range of feeling is exactly what we we're looking for in our fruit. The wider the range, the better the wine.

'You see, it's the acidic bloom of intense depravity that gives our brand its potency, its depth – we growers refer to it as *pourriture noble* – the Noble Rot – and the sweetness of finer feeling, such as love, gives it balance.

'But, knowing precisely when to halt the fermentation process the real secret of good wine. This new batch will bubble away for an aeon or so and, when fully matured, will be correctly blended, then encapsulated, labelled and exported to the far corners of the Universe. As you know, wine is a very sought after luxury, because we angels have no passion, no emotion, and we do like to experience it occasionally.'

'But what makes your particular label so popular, so special?'

'Ah! I think it's the subtle balance of opposites we achieve through our blending process. We mix lust, greed and hatred and counter-balance it with just a soupcon of high ideals, cultural aspirations and only a touch of sweetness. That's what gives our label its distinct quality and piquancy.'

'Absolutely fascinating! Well, I'd better report back, so I really must be on my way...'

'Of course, but before you go, would you like one for the road?'

11
PSYCHO-VR

JASON PULLED OFF the helmet in panic.

'Shit, man! That was scary. So real, I thought I was there. Where'd all that horror stuff come from?'

'From you, dude! It's supposed to be like that, so get used to it. The system's picking up energy patterns from your subconscious, converting them to digital and relaying them into the VR program via our software – that's all you, man – your mood, underlying anxieties, repressed stuff, whatever. You wanna try again?'

'Not sure... can you control it, you know, choose what happens?'

'Well, yes and no... you can start by thinking of something like a nice day on the beach, or the first time you got laid, but when it starts accessing the deep material, it can get pretty weird... There's always the escape button if you can't hack it. But if you wanna learn something about yourself, you have to go with the flow.'

'How does it work?'

'Dunno, man. We discovered it by accident and my department's working like crazy to work it all out. My boss thinks we'll get the Nobel Prize if we can suss it – or become a millionaires. But it's pretty cool, better than acid. and faster than therapy. Better warn you, it can, er... alter you a bit. You know, make you see things differently after a session? Sometimes you come out, er, kinda altered. You know, behaving differently and that?'

Jason gingerly put the headset on again, and settled down into the padded seat...

He is lying on his back in his cot. The room is white, a window open, net curtains fluttering in the breeze. Above him hangs a colourful mobile. He is experimenting, trying to work out if moving his legs makes the mobile dance. Each time a kick and a movement coincide, laughter detonates in his gut, washing over his body. His laughter surprises him and makes him laugh even more. His mother bustles into view, lifts and carries him to the bathroom, lays him on a hard, cold surface and roughly strips off his top and nappy then plunges him into a bath of cool water. Shock; instantaneous mood change; fear, discomfort, panic...

A wail of anguish tears from his throat..

Orange flash. He is sitting at the kitchen table, using his finger to scrape up and eat the remaining smears of cake mix from a mixing bowl. Across the room, his mother stoops low to place a cake tin in the oven, a waft of rising hot air misting her glasses.

'Mummy,' he asks plaintively, 'Why doesn't Daddy come home any more?'

His mother pauses over the oven, shuts the door and turns to him. He sees her mascara has run, and a tear is coursing down her cheek.

'Oh, darling,' she cries, moving to him, gathering him in her arms. 'I'm so sorry. Daddy's gone away, for good.'

'Why?'

'He doesn't love us anymore.'

Another flash. Jason squirmed in his seat. His world shifts to Panavision. He is in a wood, can smell the vegetation, see the dancing, dappled sunlight spotlighting circling midges, hear the breeze-rustled leaves. He becomes aware of sitting on a river bank, Tanya next to him. The water ripples and gurgles, froths and eddies; green fronds stretch and wave downstream.

'Will you be my girlfriend?' he asks, continuing to splash his feet rhythmically up and down in the cold water.

'If you like...'

The sun is warm on his skin. He feels happy.

School playground. Cold. Overcast sky. Two friends approach.

'Jason. Quick! Tanya's snogging Taylor by the bike sheds...'

A scream rips his throat...

Hospital Ward. Jason in bed, his leg encased in plaster, raised at forty-five degrees by ropes and pulleys.

'This young chap has totally wrecked his anterior cruciate ligament,' a white-coated consultant is telling a group of students gathered round the bed. 'You're a footballer, I see,' he says, turning to Jason.

'Yeah, just signed for Spurs. Start at the academy next week; going to be a pro...'

'Well, young man. I'm afraid that is not going to happen. You'll be lucky to walk without a limp, let alone play football again...'

He is engulfed by a deep sadness. It all seems so unfair...

Jason removed the helmet and laid it gently by his side. There were tears in his eyes.

He stood and walked to the door.

'You alright, man?'

'Yeah. Never better. See what you mean... feel different, changed. Got some things to sort out... See you later, man.'

He cycled across town to a house he knew well, walked up the path and knocked on the door.

'Jason! wassup, dude?'

'You borrowed my i-Pod about three months ago.'

'Oh, yeah, I...'

'I want it back – now.'

'Uh... I don't know where. it is, man. Look, I'm busy right now. Just come back some other time, will ya...'

Jason gripped the youth's shirt front and pushed him up against the wall, pressing his face close to the other's.

'NOW!'

'Okay, okay! I'll go get it. Jesus, man! What the fuck's come over you all of a sudden?'

12
THE CHOOSING

SOMETHING WASN'T RIGHT. Riku couldn't put his finger on it, but sensed things weren't quite as they should be, which was strange, he thought, because he'd been so happy these last five years since joining Seventh Heaven. He knew it wasn't nervousness; he didn't have 'butterflies', and he enjoyed interviews, usually did well... It was more a feeling of foreboding.

'Basically,' he told himself, 'I'm scared.'

Riku was on the London bound express on his way to an interview at the Church of Seventh Heaven's National Headquarters for a position as Marketing Director. If he got the job, it would mean a virtual doubling of his salary and he'd get to work with like-minded people in the fastest growing church in the world.

'The chance of a golden future – so why am I feeling so weird?' he wondered, staring down through the window at the tracks whistling by, simulating a hard-edged abstract painting. He tried closing his eyes and sidestepping the feeling – the C7H technique for overcoming anything considered negative emotion.

'What was it our founder said? "If you're not feeling happy and contented, you're in the grip of your base energies..." Maybe those energies don't want me to get this job. They always try to keep you small, confined, so I'm told. Yeah! That's it. They're what's making me feel scared. Well, I won't let that happen; they're not going to hold me back anymore.'

Continuing with the 'Think Happy, Feel Happy' exercise, Riku shifted into daydreaming mode and imagined buying that Alfa Spyder he'd always dreamed of, if he got the job, and the fat salary and the move to London and a new girlfriend, perhaps; a fiancée, a C7H wedding, many children, a forever-after-happy C7H life and...

'No – *when* I get the job,' he corrected himself.

He walked into the interview room and ritually hugged the two men and two women present – two hands behind the other's back, head over the right shoulder, then the left – and took the chair indicated.

'Right, Riku – that's your Seventh Heaven name, I assume?'

'That's right – for over three years now I got it direct from Founder

Visionary Elijah.'

'And you were initiated, what, five years ago?'

Riku nodded agreement.

'And I see from your application that you are already a Parish Aid?

'Yes. I've witnessed several hundred initiations so far.'

'Impressive for one so young...'

'Thank you.'

'What is the main precept of the Seventh Heaven Church?' one of the men threw at him.

'Er... "Submission to the Universal Energy ruling all".'

'And what do we submit?' asked the other.

'Our negativity, mainly.'

'Such as?'

'Sadness, fear, hatred, criticism, self-denigration... anything that closes down that Seventh Heaven feeling of happiness and the joy of being alive – as a member of the Church, of course...'

'I see you read our Founder's talks...' the first smiled at Riku, who nodded back, feeling sheepish, but pleased with himself and his answers so far.

'And why do you want to work for Seventh Heaven?' asked one of the women.

'I like our people – we've all got so much in common; and I believe in the Church and know in my heart that it can change society for the better the bigger it grows. And because it's a force for good in the world and it's what The Spirit ordains, of course,' Riku gushed. Then he shrugged and said. 'I'm totally committed and I just want to help Founder Visionary Elijah's mission in any small way I can, and be part of that worldwide outreach and spread, I guess. That's it, really.'

'Good answer,' the woman smiled.

After going through Riku's CV, they asked him if he had any questions. He hadn't, so they told him to step outside while they considered. Riku knew this meant they would quieten themselves, summon up the Seventh Heaven inner vibe and then ask The Spirit out loud, 'Is Riku the right person for this job?'

They would then observe their feelings – rising happiness would indicate 'yes' – any other emotion, including a feeling of emptiness, would indicate he was not the right candidate. This was the Church of Seventh Heaven's way of doing business and the basis on which it was structured, staffed, organised and run. Being guided by The Spirit in all things – a true theocracy they claimed, and liked to think.

'We are delighted to offer you the job,' they told him after summoning him back. 'When can you start?'

Riku's rise through the ranks was exceptionally rapid. Within a year he had graduated to being a Regional Aid, someone considered as an advanced spiritual being, and he was one of the youngest to have ever achieved such a position. Thus, when he got the call to attend a session to decide if he were to be further promoted – to National Level – he was not surprised. Neither could he avoid the rather smug feeling that he would become one of the top six members of the Church's inner circle in the UK – a fully-fledged, Seventh Heaven Bishop with a capital 'B'.

'Next stop International, eh?' he smiled to himself. 'Yeah, maybe, one day. Correction; *definitely* one day!''

The opportunity came sooner than even he realised it could.

'You'll be attending the World Congress in the US, I assume?' one of his female Bishop counterparts asked a few years later as they walked towards the Worship Hall in the Church's National Centre, ready to lead the evening's free-form happiness session.

'Spirit willing.'

'Good. You know there's a vacancy on the World Council, and they're asking for nominations?'

'Yes. I heard.'

'Well, we're nominating you.'

'No – really? Are you sure…?'

Riku exalted inside. This meant he would be personally interviewed by Founder Visionary Elijah – the man who had created the church after receiving a series of visions and revelations some thirty years ago. And if successful, he would become one of the twelve World Archbishops, a member of the ruling élite.

And all within ten years of initiation…

His happiness session that night was the strongest and most worshipful he had ever experienced as he danced around the hall with a spontaneous chant of well-being and laughter bubbling from his mouth, harmonising with the congregation of over a thousand free-form worshippers.

The months leading to the Congress went by in a daze and each time Riku thought of the implications of being a church leader, a ball of happiness rose and detonated in his chest forcing him to close his eyes to experience the elation in full.

'Power, travel, expenses, the wife I seek; and pure bliss, always the bliss, the joy. I was born for this,' he told himself. 'Chosen! Thank You, Great Spirit, thank You...'

The day came when, after a week at Congress, Riku got the call. Feeling nervous and unable to control the rising emotion, he was ushered into a darkened room to kneel before Founder Visionary Elijah to be examined.

Riku had seen Elijah pass by in the back of his Rolls Royce; observed him giving talks to the faithful in five-thousand seater halls; been in his presence as part of a delegation, and was aware this well-built, but corpulent, clean-shaven Afro-American was swooned over by Seventh Heaven women worldwide, but he was not prepared for the sheer presence of the man, the overwhelming charisma. Without thinking, Riku automatically prostrated himself on the floor in front of where the Founder sat.

'Riku, are you totally committed to Seventh Heaven? Will you dedicate your life to our Church?' Elijah asked in a rich, mellifluous voice.

'Yes, Visionary Founder, totally willing,' he managed to whisper.

'Get back on your knees and close your eyes. I want you to be very quiet and attentive. Ignore anything that goes on around you. I shall enter a receiving state in order for something to be revealed through me, to you; this will not be in words, but in feeling and understanding. You must weigh up what you receive, then make a life defining choice...'

Riku levered himself up onto his knees as requested and, eyes firmly closed, became aware of Elijah's deep and sonorous breathing, of the light levels changing in the room, as though all was pulsating and glowing. He sensed a presence all around him and within him, a grip on his emotional centre, then on his body, and he was transfixed, unable to move.

'This feeling...' he thought briefly. 'Holiness...?' and he gasped at the realisation.

Wordless information began to flow into his understanding, interpreted through his thinking mind.

'We are the entity Aloi,' a voice seemed to say. 'We have no physical form. You cannot see us or touch us; you can only sense us. We exist everywhere and nowhere, but because we too need food in order to exist, we travel from planet to planet seeking out psychic energy as our sustenance.

'We infiltrate the inner world of any receptive, sentient being and, when we touch, are invariably perceived as a visitation from what you call "God"; this manifests as an epiphany, a receiving, a vision – whatever corresponds to that individual's cultural and religious mythology. We then allow that receptive being the power to create a movement, a church, a cult, along with the ability to transmit, to pass on to others a rudimentary contact with us.

'Thus we establish a bridgehead preparing for our invasion.

'We sense your shock, but do not fear – our invasion is benign. We only take over the minds and inner natures of those who are willing to surrender their selves, those who are willing to allow us to reside in their body and to feed off their spiritual energy.

'In return, we give them the peace, happiness and certainty that all beings seek through their originally contrived religious faith.

'All so-called religion is simply a symbiotic relationship between an individual, or group, and ourselves. However, it is not a parasitical relationship as such, it is a true symbiosis; we do not kill or weaken our hosts; it remains in our interests to keep them alive, healthy, thriving and happy. For the more contented they are, the more nutritious is our food.

'We now offer you a choice, as we have done to countless beings on innumerable planets since time began. Accept us, become us and throw off your human-ness with all its failings – its animal nature with coarse emotions, drives, desires and passions; its decline into illness, old age and death – and experience the life-eternal, the life of bliss with us, through us.

'Refuse us and the offer we make, in your case to be our emissary and a world church leader, will be rescinded and we will bother you no more. We will even wipe your memory clean of this examination.

'Attempts to inform those outside are always met with ridicule and scorn, regardless; no one would ever believe you. It is pointless to try.

'Now you must make your decision. Back to your old self and the whims of chance, the vagaries of fortune, or a guaranteed, glorious future as a leader of our "church" on planet Earth.

'We will give you a moment alone to weigh up our offer...'

Riku, came to as he was momentarily released from the Aloi's spiritual grip. Contradictory thoughts flooded his mind.

'So, it comes down to this. Seventh Heaven is an invasion from outer space... They want to take over the world. Horrible, disgusting thought – but they offer so much...

'Do I want to go back to being Rick Smith, a nobody, a failure? Do I really want to give up my status in the Church, my chance to be a leader? Lose my happiness, my sense of well-being – all I've achieved? Don't think so... But, on the other hand, could I, should I, give up my free will, my humanity, my birthright? Do I want to be a slave to these... creatures, spirits, whatever they are? What to do? What to do?'

Then clarity. Suddenly he knew what he really wanted, what was right; there was only one choice, and he lifted his head and cried out from his innermost depths.

'I... choose... *Aloi*!'

13
THE SUIT

HMM! WHY DID I suddenly curtail my career with the International Space Agency and end up doing this? Good question – and rather a long answer...

I suppose it started during the first Jupiter Mission, back in 2060, do you remember? No? Well it was newsworthy at the time because of the so-called flying suits we wore – they were technological miracles in their day but, like all technology, they were prone to malfunctions.

Now, as I recall, the plan for this first manned scientific mission to Jupiter was that the mothership, Methuselah 4, would remain in geostationary orbit and we (a team of three specialist pilots) would descend into different layers of the planet's atmosphere to record weather extremes, monitor wind speeds, electrical storm activity, look for possible life and so on. I wasn't a scientist, by the way – more a gofer.

The suits we wore were mini, one-man space stations, and fully self-contained, because we were going to be living in them for over a year. They'd been tailor-made to fit our individual, specific metabolic and physical make-ups and had cost millions of dollars each.

They were about the size of a small car, but egg-shaped with stubby wings. Each unit had an anti-grav drive housed at the rear, with the suit's computer system and cabin up front.

The power unit not only provided propulsion but also generated power for the recycling of oxygen and keeping temperature and pressure at Earth levels. The computer supplied food and drink, comms and entertainment and organised the disposal of waste and so on – all mod cons, as they say.

At the 'cloud tops', or what we see as the surface, the temperature of Jupiter is minus 145 degrees C, but as you descend through the layers, temperatures increase with atmospheric pressure. At the level we were going to be working, the pressure is 10 times that of Earth, but the temperature is around room temperature at 20 C. But it wouldn't be advisable to open your door! The atmosphere at that level consists of nothing but ammonia and methane and whips round the planet at over 500 miles per hour. But, if 'life as we know it', or can recognise it, existed on Jupiter, that's where we'd find it.

The outward bound journey went smoothly (and pretty boringly) – the fusion drives getting us there in a year from take off to parking in orbit. Then we three explorers, Captain Bob Newhart, Flight Lieutenant Gary Oldham and myself, prepared ourselves for the mission.

Our cabins were no bigger than the cockpit of a small car, and jam-packed with technology; and, because we would literally be sitting down for a year, the 'smart seats' we sat in had been built from a special, nano-computerised foam that not only prevented contact sores, but exercised our limbs while we worked and slept, as well as attending to our personal hygiene.

This system was backed up by ingested nano-computers, hundreds of them, which constantly monitored our bodies and their individual metabolisms, alerting the main system to dietary deficiencies, potential illness and infections, any build ups of toxins, all that kind of stuff. They also controlled our stress levels, even our sleep patterns – they did everything needed to keep us fit and healthy and in first class working order.

In front of us were heads up screens displaying what the cameras saw – there were no viewing ports. The hull, in order to survive the heat and pressure, could have no surface projections or breaks in its integrity (we were literally sealed in). In fact the hulls had been constructed from a newly created material that was as light and malleable as plastic, but stronger than iridium and could survive temperatures of up to 5,000 Kelvin and pressures of hundreds of tons per square inch.

The control panels for flight manoeuvrability, measurement making, suit controls and comms were ergonomically built around us – everything logical and within easy reach. The main system computer could continue working while we slept, constantly monitoring and reporting back to the mother ship.

So, we were carefully fitted into our flying suits, which were essentially extensions of our bodies; all tests were made, checks done, and then we were successfully launched.

I cannot explain the joy of surfing the Jovian clouds – let's just say I was in paradise (and I could hear the whoops and delighted laughter from my team-mates over the comms). We'd all flown supersonic jets and been to the Moon and Mars and back as pilots, and trained for this on remarkably accurate simulators, but nothing compared to, or prepared us for, the reality.

I guess, like all things, the novelty wore off after a few days and we settled down to the year long task ahead.

And then, after a few months, something went horribly wrong with my suit.

To this day, the boffins aren't sure what it was. Opinions vary from a feasible collapsed micro-rivet through to a Jovian life form sabotaging the vessel (unlikely – we found no recognisable 'life' during the mission – but you never know...).

Basically, the main computer went haywire, first putting me into a coma and then diving down into the atmosphere heading for depths well beyond the mission limits.

Now, if you continue to descend into Jupiter, the temperature and pressure increase dramatically. Once you hit the liquid hydrogen layer at 20,000 miles the temperature is 10,000 Kelvin and the pressure would crush our moon to the size of a pea.

The first thing I knew about it was a high-pitched whine in my headset – Mission Control trying to wake me up.

'Chick One, do you copy, come in please... Chick One, do you copy,' over and over....

I managed to pull out of sleep and respond, and then I learned that I was in a decaying orbit and had about five days before I hit the 'crushing zone'.

It was then I realised that I had no control, that the computer was unresponsive, yet working away like it had gone rogue. I was explaining this to them and then, suddenly they were out of contact range.

The next orbit was probably the worst I had to contend with, knowing my possible fate now, and that I couldn't do a thing about it. Jupiter is approx. 250,000 miles in circumference – the distance to the moon from Earth – and I was orbiting it in a day and there was no way they could reach me when I was on the far side.

Next time round, they came up with a series of tests and reconfigurations – they couldn't even send me a text message, they said – the computer blocked it out as junk!

This went on for another 3 days; information, tests, checks, reconfigurations, interspersed with the long periods of isolation...

Finally, I was on my last orbit, and again out of contact range. If I didn't get control back with their next and final instructions, that was it.

The imminence of one's death certainly gets you thinking, and with twelve hours to go I felt like a condemned man in his cell waiting and hoping for the Governor's reprieve. At some point, I went into a reverie and realised something which, frankly, changed my life...

I perceived my situation as a metaphor for human life. I saw that my real, eternal self cannot live in this material environment without some form of survival suit. This suit – known as a body – was analogous to the one I was in, hurtling towards Jupiter's surface and destruction, in that it too is autonomous; but, just as I had no control, neither does my real self, my soul, have any over my human body.

Somehow, when I was born, something went wrong and my real self, my soul, lost it, or went into a coma, or whatever happens to souls... But the body-suit goes on performing, just as it was programmed to – I grew up, learned a language, went to school, met a girl, married and raised a family, all the usual stuff, but the body-suit was out of my control and led me eventually into disaster. In my case, it was my string of extra-marital affairs and subsequent divorce; and then my little gambling habit I'd picked up after, and so on. No need to go into detail... suffice to say I was a wreck.

Then it occurred to me that this is what our prophets have been trying to get across over the millennia in all the holy books – that there's a mission control out there, and it is constantly trying to waken our real selves and will help us get back in control of our suits, and out of danger, if only we'd listen. At that moment, I felt the calling.

An epiphany, you say? Perhaps, but all I knew and wanted at that moment was to tell the whole world, somehow.

Then, 'Mission control to Chick One,' interrupted my thoughts, 'Do you receive? Over.'

'Loud and clear,' I replied, laughing, aware of the double irony. 'We haven't much time now. We're going to get you to do one last series of checks on the alpha sub-routines; first, hold down systems check button and press enable...'

I cannot express the relief I felt as, an hour later, the suit's screens flickered, pulsed and then finally came on-stream with all functions normal. Within seconds, I had control and was sweeping back up though the layers and out into space, heading for the mothership...

But I'd had my wake-up call, and knew my life would never be the same. And when I got back to earth, I resigned my commission, left NASA and applied to join a seminary...

Yes, I'll be there in just a minute...

I'm sorry, you'll have to excuse me. Perhaps we can finish this later? They're waiting for me – I have to go and serve Mass now...

14
THE VALE OF TEARS

I'M RECORDING THIS from my holding cell. They said I could leave a closure message 'to whom it might concern', but as I can't for the life of me think of anyone who might actually be concerned, I doubt this message will ever be heard.

I'm flawed, you see. I committed a crime. A crime so heinous that it threatened the stability of our egalitarian, perfectly balanced, 'one in spirit' society, blah, blah, blah. I hacked into the forbidden knowledge database... And, as I knew I would, I got found out.

So, knowing that, why did I do it, you might ask? Because it *was* forbidden, I suppose, and because I *enjoyed* it.

Now, I'm going to pay for my indiscretion. I had no defence, you see. A spike of euphoria showed up on my emotional record, precisely coinciding with the moment of the act. It was no surprise, therefore, when the Court re-manifested after their deliberations and pronounced me 'Guilty in the first degree'.

What was a shock, though, was the severity of the sentence. I'd expected reprogramming, or some form of long-term therapy, with a public humiliation thrown in perhaps as a warning to other potential miscreants. But the Court took it really seriously and called for banishment. I'm such an abomination, I'm to be stripped down, dismantled and cast out.

They'll take me to a lab some time soon, where they'll wipe my mind, deactivate my personality and separate what's left of my self from my entity. Then they'll mix my remaining 'essence' with synthetic, carbon-based DNA and despatch it as biological seed to a prison ship orbiting a star somewhere on the far side of the galaxy.

What scares me most is that my essence is to be divided, and my two halves will have to exist as gender-opposites with only finite, mammalian bodies as a support structure, which means we'll have disease, old age and death to contend with...

Not only that, the prison ship is governed by a crude 'survival of the fittest' evolutionary process, so in order to survive, I, we – and our biologically produced descendants – must strive for sentience, a fully functioning brain, language and basic technology in as few generations as we can possibly manage. If we don't make it, we end up as merely part of the food chain – prey to all the indigenous predators on board.

Apparently, there are so many pitfalls in any evolutionary process... if we don't get food production sorted, we'll starve and die out; if we overproduce, we'll use up all the inherent resources and burn, freeze or suffocate to death; if we become over-technological we'll wipe ourselves out with wars, our competitive mammalian natures forever seeking territory and dominance over others... The sad, suffering lot of biological entities, I suppose. No wonder they call the prison ship 'The Vale of Tears'.

The reality is, I'm being sent back to the level my species started from many, many aeons ago, and the evolutionary pattern I must set in motion is to enable my descendants to eventually become a fully evolved, one-in-spirit being again; this is the only way I can purge my faults and be accepted back into society, they tell me.

And it's not going to be easy. Apart from the problems I've just mentioned, I've only got about ten billion orbits to re-achieve this status before the local star burns out and absorbs everything in its system, including the ship. And that's a blip compared to the time scales I'm used to.

To sum up, if I don't get it right, I will never return here; I'll simply cease to exist – oblivion, finally and forever.

I wish they hadn't told me all this, I've turned purple with terror, but knowing what's to transpire in detail is part of the punishment, I'm assured.

The Court also told me that the theory behind my punishment is that they believe a society that has produced an anomaly simply cannot move on until things are put right. They say it's like a complex calculation that won't resolve. You have to go back to find and correct what is wrong before you can ever get a right answer. And, in this calculation, I am the anomaly, the mistake...

My escort has arrived – time to go. Wish me luck and think of me occasionally. Soon, I'll be an Algorithmically Deconstructed Amorphic Mutation. You can just call me Adam for short...

15
COMMUNIQUÉ

To all sentient beings on Earth.

We, the inhabitants of the planet you call Neptune, are recently in receipt of your probe, which we cannot return as it has disintegrated and been absorbed into the molecular structure of our planet.

Whilst we appreciate the gesture, we wish to communicate that we desire no further contact with your species.

We do not send this message in a spirit of unfriendliness, but wish to point out that communication between us is almost impossible. You are a carbon based life form, currently in 'biological' mode, whereas we, originally an ammonia based life form, have long since evolved into one transcendent being existing on the plane of pure consciousness.

Consequently, it has taken enormous resources to interpret your probe, divine your technologies and language construction in order to send this communiqué in the form of binary radio pulses – we have not used comparable technology for over a billion of your Terran years. In fact, science and technology play no part in our lives, which is replete with culture and the arts

We do, however, feel we owe you an explanation. We did in fact visit your planet two billion Earth years ago, when we too were in 'scientific' mode, naively believing that exploring the physical universe would lead to answers concerning the structure and origins of the creation and, therefore, the true nature of reality.

As an experiment, we seeded the rudimentary animal beings then inhabiting your planet with the potential for developing culture, science and technology. Unfortunately, the carbon based life forms, as we later came to understand, have a tendency to create exponential technological growth but, because of an innate, competitive animal nature, they use it aggressively for personal and societal power struggles, particularly over territory and energy. Such greed invariably leads to wars of self-extinction. (In fact, the disappearance of your dinosaur species was not due to a large meteor strike, as you currently surmise, but to the waging of a catastrophic biological war. These creatures were much more intelligent than you assume, because you tend to relate intelligence with brain size – a common misconception throughout the galaxy.)

We have long since abandoned such fruitless experiments, along with the quest for 'knowledge', realising it is inappropriate to meddle with evolutionary forces and that the answers we sought are unknowable – no creation can ever 'understand' its creator.

Your kind must now find its own way, but we hope that, over the next billion years, you might survive, and that you will, through natural evolutionary development, eventually outgrow your biological mode to become a transcendent unity, which is the ultimate goal of all self-aware species.

We wish you 'bon voyage', while expecting no further contact from you, nor response to this communiqué until such time as you are fully matured.

Fare well
The Neptunians

16

DEVIL-MAY-CARE

I'VE NEVER VISITED First Earth and never will. I'm fourth generation Terranovan, my great, great grand parents emigrating here over a hundred and fifty years ago to this habitable (but then uninhabited) planet in the Alpha Centuri system. I've seen the educational pictures at school, of course, and heard all about First Earth society in Cultural History lessons, but it all meant little to me. And anyway, the old place is ruined by now. Dry, arid, the climate gone to pot, or so my Grandad tells me. He said it was mostly because of rampant greed over energy resources, the self-interested denial of climate change by the ruling élites and their pseudo-scientific belief in 'the balance of nature'.

'What a laugh!' he said. 'Nature's wild, son. Rain forests don't grow back, lakes don't refill; chemicals pumped into the atmosphere don't go away. Nope, everything entropies to desert in the end if you continually use it and abuse it.

'And our Founding Fathers decided they weren't going to let all that happen again on Terranova,' he said, slapping his thigh for emphasis.

At school I learned that the original two thousand settlers came with little in the way of technology, bringing only hand tools and simple weapons for hunting and defence, a library of approved books and basic medicine and agricultural kits. They even dismantled their spacecraft, stockpiling the metals for later conversion to tools, but ripping out and burning all the electronics and plastics, as well as burying the fusion drives that got them here in three decades.

They wanted a return to the simple life, and became hewers of wood, drawers of water and tillers of the soil, totally eschewing science and technology for good. Technology is the work of the Devil, the Elders say. They based our future society on the Amish back on First Earth (except we're allowed bone buttons, now that all the zips and Velcro have worn out, thank the Good Lord).

It was going to be a brave new world; everybody equal, no élites, no power struggles, no exploitation, living in harmony with nature, a heaven on Terranova.

'Trouble is,' my Grandad confided, 'they brought the Bible with them.'

My Grandad says we live as, and are intellectually equivalent to, a

Middle-Ages village society back on First Earth. But he has to be careful in what he says.

'The walls have ears, lad,' he tells me often. But, because he trusts me, he goes on, 'That so-called "Good Book" with its belief in Heaven and Hell and the war between good and evil has done for us. Our lives are riddled with angels and spirits and the Devil and all his minions. All this half-baked, religious mumbo-jumbo does is make us like superstitious tribesmen; peasants scared of our own shadows. We believe in eternal damnation, in purgatory and ghosts and ghouls and demons, good luck charms, talismans. Not forgetting the idols – the crucifixes, the icons of saints, the concept of original sin – a world of Christian juju and it's ruined our lives here.'

And I begin to see his point – a glimmer of understanding coming through. Strewth! If anyone ever found these writings, me and Grandad would be hauled before the Elders on charges of blasphemy and heresy – and if we didn't recant and beg forgiveness, it'd be exorcism for us both; months of isolation, near starvation and regular whippings and scourgings until we were 'purified' and deemed fit to return to society as proper 'God-fearing folks', Satan well and truly driven out.

Yeah, you've guessed it, we're rebels, free-thinkers, agnostics, apostates – or more simply, people who think there should be more to life than living like old First Earth, red-neck, Bible-bashing hicks.

I'm sensibly covert right now – not having met anyone else who thinks like me and Grandad so far. That doesn't mean they're not around, just that the smart thing to do is to keep dissent to yourself, unless you're absolutely sure of the person you're talking to. Grassing people up, even family, for 'retro-thought' is encouraged by the Elders. They run a tight ship and certainly don't want non-conformists anywhere near the helm.

Here on Terranova, when you get to fifteen, you leave home and have to live in the Longhuts – single-sex dorms, eight to a room. For three years, you learn your craft – animal husbandry or arable farming; carpentry or metalwork; civic construction or mining; miscellaneous, but essential, production work – or you train to be a doctor, teacher or vicar, depending on your gift (usually determined by your physique and the Elders' staffing needs). The women get the choice between baby-rearing and domestic skills (cooking, sewing, weaving, housewifery), or nursing and midwifery – seems an awful waste of resources to me, but it's what the Bible ordains, the Elders pronounce.

By the way, we've abolished money. Every one gets an entitlement of basic rights – food and clothes and somewhere to live according to marital status and size of family. You can barter for extras, like this notebook and pencil I'm using, by doing some gardening or woodcutting for a maker of what you want; but it's not allowed to hoard or overdo it – you'll be up in front of the Elders if you do. 'Trading is the work of the Devil,' they insist, 'Man shall live by his labour alone, working for the good of the common weal, given only his needs, not his wants; money is the root of all evil etc, etc...'

The other night the guys in my room were chatting and mucking around, cracking jokes and telling stories, as normal, but the conversation turned to ghosts and demons. Stories handed down from grandmas and grandpas were told and the atmosphere got creepier and creepier, some of the guys getting pretty scared. One guy said his Gran had told him that if you talk about ghosts and spirits, you attract them. At that moment, a window blew open and a gust of wind blew the oil lamps out, and we all shrieked, and one or two of the younger guys burst into tears. Everyone got pretty shook up at this.

Being one designated as teacher, I'm kinda looked up to as the leader, so I had to step in and wind things up.

'C'mon, guys, that's enough of this. Time for bed. Say your prayers and ask the good angels for protection.'

I no longer believe in the power of prayer, or the concept of angels, of course, good or bad, but I have to play my role and keep my opinions to myself.

Later, I lay in bed unable to sleep, my mind going round and round in circles. Although rebellious by nature and lapping up Grandad's heretical views, I had undergone a brainwashing, religious education for the last twenty years, so I was, to be honest, a little mixed up.

Is it all true, all that stuff we hear in church on a Sunday morning? Are the Elders right, is there a heaven and a hell? Will I get punished for my apostasy, both in this world and the next? Am I a doubting Thomas? Are there angels and demons battling for my eternal soul? Are my rebellious thoughts evidence of the Devil at work in me? How could I know for sure? How could the Elders, and everyone around me for that matter, be so certain, so dogmatic about anything?

My mind was in turmoil, then an idea dropped in, a way I could maybe find out the truth...

* * *

It was around 2 o'clock in the morning when I arrived in the forest clearing, about three miles from our village. Both moons were up, each in half phase, so it was light, but not overbright.

As I planned, I stood at the centre of the clearing and asked out loud, 'If there are devils and demons, ghosts and ghouls, spirits and genies, come and get me now!'

Silence. 'Come on, Mr. Devil! If you exist, come and take me right now! Show yourself...'

Nothing stirred. Nothing happened.

After five minutes, I decided this was enough, I'd had my answer, I'd got my proof – it was all moonshine. So I began to walk back home.

I'd gone about a mile, when I heard the report of a hunter's shotgun. Then another and another. Probably a poacher, I thought, out after rabbits. Then a sudden thought; supposing he sees me moving through the trees and thinks I'm a bear...?

A sickening fear welled up.

'Shit! Gotta get out of here, fast!' and I began to run.

Another report and panic overwhelmed me and I ran and ran in sheer terror, whimpering with fear, my breath rasping in the cold night air. As I ran, I imagined the slug ripping into my body, ricocheting inside, severing arteries, smashing into vital organs, breaking bones (I'd been allowed to hunt with my Grandad, and knew what a mess those old twelve-bores made of an animal's hide). I have truly never been so scared as I was that night, as I ran and ran and ran....

Eventually, I reached the edge of the wood and slowed down, panting and shivering in a cold sweat. A while later, I slid through the back streets of the village to get to my dorm, carefully aware of the nightly curfew.

I tip-toed in and crawled into bed, drew up the blankets and lay there, totally shocked at what had transpired.

Then realisation dawned. Now I really know the truth.

There are no demons, ghouls, jinns and devils out there. They're all inside. We conjure them all up from our imaginations and fears, and then project them onto gnarled trees, lumpen rocks, clouds and lightning, anything out of the norm, anything we don't understand. They are as our own shadows following us around.

There's no Devil incarnate out there, stalking us, trying to trick us into evil, fighting for our very souls as our Elders dictate.

So, I think, does he then live inside each one of us? Is he the sum total of our fears, our hatreds, our prejudices, our superstitions? Not quite, I tell myself. For just as cold is the absence of heat, and dark the absence of light, so is ignorance the absence of understanding and hatred the absence of love. And without understanding and love there can be no compassion.

Therefore, if the so-called 'Devil' is just that absence, that ignorance, that lack of compassion, then the Devil is... nothing; no thing at all...

17
SELF-GOOGLED

HUSSEIN CARMICHAEL WAS at a loose end. His live-in partner was away for ten days, visiting her parents, and he'd just sent off a document he'd prepared for a client and now had nothing to do until supper; so he opened his browser, typed his name into Google and clicked 'search'.

Sharing a name with the President of the United States didn't help. With 36,000,000 links, page after page came up with a variety of Carmichaels linked to Barack Hussein Obama – from Hoagy to the King of Jordan (and not forgetting a former Iraqi leader). But he pressed on regardless in a zombie-like trance.

Around page fifty, his own name jumped out at him. Intrigued, he clicked the link, which took him to the website of a graphic designer. There were no other clues about this other Hussein Carmichael, but there was a contact email address.

Out of interest, he decided to shoot off an e-mail:

> Hi Hussein
> I saw your name – our name – on Google & visited your site (very impres-
> sive). Would you be interested in swapping info? Just seemed odd to me
> that there are two of us living in the UK. Over to you, if interested.
> Hussein

He clicked send, switched his laptop to sleep mode, grabbed his coat, went out for supper and promptly forgot the email he'd just sent.

Two days later, he was surprised to see, in his junkmail, a reply from Hussein Carmichael.

> Hi Hussein
> Fascinating, indeed. A quick bio from me: I'm 34, and a designer. Married,
> no kids yet. I live in Finsbury Park and work near Russell Square for a
> large design group (studied graphics at the University of Kent). Mother
> Iranian, married a Scot, hence the name. How about yours?
> Hussein

He couldn't believe the coincidences and immediately hit 'reply' and emailed back:

Hi Hussein
Unbelievable! I'm also 34 and my mother was Iranian and she married a
Scot as well. Not only that, I live and work in London – commuting
Clapham to St. Pauls 5 days a week. I'm a solicitor, though, read law at
Edinburgh. My God! We must do lunch. Can you suggest a day during the
week?
Hussein

A couple of days later, Hussein the solicitor was standing outside
the Costa close to Holborn underground station, waiting for Hussein
the designer. They'd agreed to meet around one pm. It was a fine day
and Hussein had opted to wait outside. He realised they hadn't
described themselves to each other, it seemed too theatrical, somehow. So, apart from a 34 year old male, he had no idea who he was
looking for.

Around one-thirty, he began to feel irritated. He searched in his
pockets for his mobile, realising with horror he had left it in his raincoat
back at the office.

'Bollocks.'

He walked into Costa again, shiftily scanning the lunchtime throng,
but saw no lone male, everyone seemed to be engaged in conversation
with a partner or in a group.

As two o'clock approached, he decided to call it a day and returned
to work in a very bad mood.

Arriving back, he collected his mobile. 'Three new message,' it
announced.

'Message timed at 1.26: Am here. Where R U? Hussein.'

'Message timed at 1.42: Still waiting...'

'Message timed at 2.02; Sorry. Gotta go. I'll email. H.'

Hussein shook his head in disbelief.

'How the hell can two so-called professionals cock up a simple meeting?' he wondered to himself.

Hi Hussein, he typed that evening, back home.
Sorry about that. I was there, but I'd stupidly left my mobile at the office.
Are you still up for a meet? This time, let's describe ourselves (and maybe
I'll wear a white carnation or something ;-)
I'm really, really sorry. Suggest another date and this time I'll bring my
mobile!
Hussein

Within half an hour, he had his reply.

> Hi Hussein
> Yeah, weird, How did we miss one another? I'd still like to meet – maybe tomorrow, same time, same place? Or the day after? You choose and send me a description or something ;-)
> HC

Two days later, Hussein was beginning to feel very uncomfortable. It was a quarter past one and again he was standing outside the same Costa, this time looking for someone of similar build and height to himself, but with long hair and a goatee beard, wearing a black leather jacket. Hussein had told the other Hussein that he, too, was six feet, twelve stone, but short haired and clean shaven and would be wearing a dark grey suit, white shirt and sober tie (the solicitor's uniform, he'd cracked).

He produced his mobile – scrolled to Hussein and pressed green.

'Hi, Hussein, where are you?'

'Yo – I'm outside Costa's – where are you?'

'Yeah I'm here. Can't see you though...'

Hussein looked rapidly from left to right, trying to spot someone on a mobile.

'Mate, I'm right in the doorway – still can't see you...'

'Shit, man – so am I...'

'You sure you're in the right Costa? At the junction of Holborn and Kingsway?'

'Of course – but where are you?'

Hussein began to feel uneasy. Had he hooked up with a nutter? Was the guy standing across the street, videoing the whole thing – and would he put it on YouTube or FaceBook and it'd go viral; seventy million hits and he'd be number one on RudeTube – the laughing stock of the whole world?

'Er... what's going on...?' he asked meekly, yet angrily convinced now that this charade was some kind of practical joke, that he was the butt, the sucker, the mark.

'You tell me, man. All I know is, I'm standing in the entrance to Costa's in High Holborn, wearing a black leather jacket like I said I would, mobile in hand and I can't see you anywhere. You sure you're in the right place?'

'Of course I am. I'm standing in the doorway and you are definitely not here...'

'This too weird, man. I'm going. I'll be in touch...' and the phone went dead.

* * *

After making 'welcome home' love, Hussein and his girlfriend lay in bed watching TV.

'Anything interesting happened while I was away?' Marie asked, snuggling up, laying her head on his shoulder.

'Funny you should ask that...' and Hussein told her the whole story to date, including the fact the two Husseins had made no further contact.

'Mmmm. Strange. We've got to get to the bottom of this. Tell you what, why don't we get in touch and arrange to meet him and his wife at the weekend?' Marie suggested. 'We've got nothing planned and it could be interesting...?'

Sunday lunchtime. Emails had been sent, phone calls made and arrangements set for a get-together at the Spaniards Inn, Hampstead.

'Great, so we'll meet around one – outside if it's fine, or in the saloon bar if wet.'

This time they had swapped photos.

'My God,' Marie had exclaimed, 'you are very similar. Same build, same black hair and skin tone – must be the Iranian in you...'

'Wow, his wife is hot,' Hussein whistled, then grunted as Marie dug him in the ribs.

'Let's hope he fancies me, too,' she laughed. 'Could make this a *very* interesting meet...'

At one-ten, Hussein could stand it no longer and called Hussein and Brigitte.

'Hi, where are you people? We're outside the pub...'

'So are we...'

Hussein went pale and turned to Marie, close to tears and shaking with an admix of rage and fear. 'It... it's happening again...'

'Give me the phone... Hi, Hussein, this is Marie. We can't see you or Brigitte anywhere. From the entrance here we can see down Spaniards End and there's only the one way in from the car park. So where are you?'

'Hi, Marie – nice to meet you. We came by taxi – we were dropped off about 5 minutes ago – we're standing outside by the main entrance. Where are you guys?'

'My God,' Marie whispered to Hussein, hand over the mouthpiece, 'he even sounds like you.' Then back to the other Hussein, 'We're here. Spaniards Inn – you definitely got the right one?'

'Sure – big white building, very old, Spaniards End, off Spaniards Road, Hampstead, London?'

'Yeah – that's the place.'

'Let's all go into the bar ...'

'Well, we're here. Still can't see you – and it's not that busy...'

'Hey – I've got an idea... Take a photo of yourselves with the bar tender and send it to me on my mobile, and we'll do the same thing...'

'Jesus! Different bartenders, but everything else looks identical.'

'Is that a Sunday paper on the table? What's the date?'

'Sunday, 7th of August 2015...'

'Yeah, the same. What's the headline?'

'Obama to send troops into Libya.'

'What's Obama?'

'You know – Barrack Obama?'

'Who?'

'President of the US?'

'But Sarah Palin's President...'

'Oh. My. God...'

* * *

'Still no news?' Hussein asked, hanging his coat in the hall and entering the lounge.

'No, nothing', Marie replied, shaking her head.

'That's over a week now. God, I hope they're OK. They were so worried about the political situation last time we spoke... North Korea invading the South, backed by China... the US sending troops. Jeez, that's a scary situation. I'd shit myself if it happened here.'

'You think they may have gone nuclear?'

'That's what I'm worried about. Especially as we only get static when we try to contact them now... And his details are no longer on the web. Christ! It can't have just ended abruptly after ten years... doesn't make sense. But, yeah, I'm thinking worse case scenario.'

'God, that's sad. Now it might be over, do you sometimes wonder if we should've, you know, told the authorities about what had happened? Not kept it to ourselves?'

'No, we discussed this. I think it was right not to. Our world would've been totally disrupted, we'd've been mere lab rats for the rest of our lives.'

'I suppose... I wonder if there are others?'

'Maybe. And maybe they came to the same conclusion – keep schtum.'

'God I miss talking to them. It was so exciting, so fascinating swapping life stories, what was going on for us, kids, work, leisure and all that – and comparing the subtle differences in our cultures, like who was in or out, what films were running, who won the World Cup, Oscar winners, all that stuff. All so close, yet just different. What a shame we could only do it electronically, that we couldn't meet face to face.'

'Would've been impossible of course – assuming our interpretation was right, that me and Hussein were, in a sense, the same person; that decisions, or rather one particular decision at a precise moment in time had made a fork in my life and each Hussein, or rather our collective mass of particles and wave forms, had drifted into two parallel worlds – identical, yet subtly different, and we could quite happily exist in two places at once. Well, that's the theory... Could've happened to you, as well, but you just haven't found out about it yet. Maybe there are hundreds of mes and yous out there. Who knows?'

'Well, I'm going to try them again... maybe it's just a glitch. Maybe their world hasn't ended...'

18
OTHER REALMS HOLIDAYS INC

Dear Customer,

Thank you for choosing Other Realms Holidays and we sincerely hope you enjoy your vacation and find it not only stimulating, but also educational.

As you may be aware, in order to exist in another realm, an accurately tailored and formatted survival unit (Biopod) is essential, and the unit supplied must be worn at all times throughout your vacation.

Attached to this document is list of Frequently Asked Questions. Please read it thoroughly before embarkation and keep in a safe, readily accessible place for further consultation on your outward bound and return journeys as well as during your vacation, in case of the unlikely event of an emergency.

Please also ensure that you are at the embarkation point at precisely the moment requested, as the timing of projection into your prefabricated Biopod awaiting you at your destination is hypercritical.

Finally, please remember that it is impossible to bring souvenirs back with you, but holiday memory-snaps may be downloaded immediately on your return and encapsulated for eternity.

It now remains for us to wish you Bon Voyage and to remind you to contact us at any time, should you have any queries or concerns not addressed in this communication.

The Management Team, Other Realms Holidays

* * *

BIOPOD FAQs

(i) What is a Biopod?

The Biopod (also referred to as a 'materiality', or 'body') is a biologically enhanceable device tailored for survival on a specific physical plane. Each unit is totally unique, but displays an admix of qualities inherited from its local progenitors.

When fully matured, the pod's inbuilt operating system ('wetware') enables a high level of consciousness through cognitive mechanisms such as thought and language and associated learning skills; trait-positive and -negative attitudes; a wide range of emotional response facilities to the local environment, and, as a bonus feature, the ability to seek, find and recognise Biopods inhabited by others holidaying in the same realm. should you wish to link up and share experiences.

(ii) How will my Biopod be delivered?
Because the physical laws of your destination prohibit manifestation as a fully-fledged being, the Biopod will be manufactured at the point of arrival. After entity projection, you will join and enter your pod at the earliest of its biological manifestation (i.e. as the first cellular unit created from the seed and ova of its 'parents'). The pod is then developed through its inherent cell-duplication process and will mature (i.e. 'grow') in accordance with the physical laws of, and input from, the environment it is designed for in a series of predetermined phases:

- PHASE1: post-projection and embryonic development
- PHASE 2: separation from the host unit
- PHASE 3: physical/cognitive development
- PHASE 4: education/character development
- PHASE 5: pair bonding/reproduction and
societal exploration/integration
- PHASE 6: full maturation/societal specialisation
- PHASE 7: Reflection/preparation for return
journey

(iii) Will I be aware of the maturation processes?
Phase 1 is usually quite painless and stress free (apart from occasional emotional disruption from the host-parent unit during embryonic development, and assuming the host unit does not become dysfunctional during this phase).

It is regrettable, however, that this first cell, while it contains all the requisite information for full biological development in the form of encoded DNA relative to the realm's elemental base, it may have been infected by viruses from the host units and/or program bugs, possibly as far back as seven generations. But, these viruses/bugs can be de-programmed by the 'style of life' adopted as the unit matures.

As the pod matures and grows in size, the inboard computer will gradually take over all sub-routines such as maintaining typical bio-functions – fuel intake and energy distribution by whatever system is natural in your chosen realm (be that photosynthetic or enzymatic, for example).

It should be noted that the transition from Phase 1 to 2 can sometimes be traumatic and cause phase-flow problems. However, this can be remedied at any time during subsequent phases simply by becoming aware of any dysfunction and seeking specialist help either from the medical profession in your holiday realm, or, if possible, by contacting our Head Office.

In phase 3, self-consciousness will develop alongside language, individual self-awareness, thought processes, a distinct 'personality' and 'character' etc., in readiness for which, the inboard computer is fully programmed.

A caveat: be aware that as the computer uploads the phase programs into functionality, your current 'self-entity' will take more and more of a back seat. At each juncture, it is essential to self-monitor and to take control and guide all interactions. Failure to do so runs the risk of serious Biopod dysfunction.

Phases 4, 5 and 6 are where the holiday really starts. By this time, the Biopod should be fully matured and operating at 100% efficiency, and the inboard computer fully programmed and running smoothly, helping in the correct choice of compatible partners (in order to produce trouble-free offspring), career satisfaction and wealth creation, including a pleasing domicile. The overall effect of these correct choices should bring mental and emotional stability, thus making your holiday a pleasant experience.

(iv) What safeguards can I make against pod malfunction?

As a simple rule, remember at all times that the key to a safe and successful holiday is moderation. Overindulgence in any of the diversions found in the other realm you are holidaying in (such as same- and inter-gender sexual activity, the imbibing of narcotics, stimulants and hallucinogenic intoxicants, the amassing of 'wealth', overindulgence in energy intake, the enjoyment of causing pain to other entities – both physical and mental and so on) will all lead eventually to pod malfunction and may well inhibit your ability to return to your home realm.

(v) What happens when the holiday ends?

The ending of your holiday begins as you move into Phase 7 and begin the process of reflection on achievement and experience along with preparation for return.

As long as the pod has been kept in good order, the appropriate, recommended fuels have been used and the computer has not been infected with viruses, or malfunctioned because of overindulgences (see item iv above), the transition from the pod back to your home base should happen automatically and extremely smoothly as the pod comes to the end of its useful life cycle and simply 'shuts down'.

However, be warned that the moment of departure cannot be precisely calculated and the suddenness and speed of its happening may leave you somewhat disoriented on arrival home, but the feeling fades very quickly

(vi) What should I do if there is a malfunction?

Don't panic! You are monitored by head office at all times. If your pod fails prematurely, or if you fail to re-manifest at the end of the holiday, you will be held in stasis while we endeavour to project a new Biopod to your location, at the same time enabling you to merge with it at the moment of its conception.

On entering the new pod, the exact same development process (Phases 1–7), as experienced during your first holiday, will be re-enacted and it is essential that, this time, you do not repeat the same behaviour patterns, which caused the previous malfunction(s). This may take several attempts, but do not despair; we can assure you that we have never 'lost' a holidaymaker thus far.

Disclaimer: Please note that failure to follow the comprehensive instructions supplied can cause both software and biomechanical hardware malfunctions, which could, over time, lead to premature system failure and immediate curtailment of your holiday. Other Realms Holidays and the Cosmopod manufacturers, therefore, accept no responsibility whatsoever for any failures, particularly if caused by the disregarding of said instructions.

19

THE LECTURE

"WELCOME TO YOU all and thank you for coming. I'm Professor Nigel Braithwaite and my lecture this evening is entitled 'Alien Abduction. True or False?'

"Well, I hope to shock you, or at least the cynics among you, by stating, yes, it's true. Alien Abduction does exist – 'in a kind of way'. Not, of course, anything like it's portrayed in the media; there are no flying saucers or spindly grey creatures with big eyes beaming you up into their spacecraft to undertake unspeakable scientific or sexual experiments on you per se – the reality is somewhat rather closer to home. But I'm getting ahead of myself.

"First, I must ask if you've you ever noticed how our comprehension of ourselves, particularly our minds and bodies, our social networks and even the universe in which we exist, relates directly to, and is informed by, the technology extant in the era in which one lives? For example, during the Ancient Era, which embraces the bronze and iron ages, right up to 500AD, when ceramics, glass making and smelting, and latterly aqueducts and under-floor heating, were state-of-the-art technology, the body's respiratory, cardiac and circulatory systems were understood in terms of pumps, bellows and furnaces. Fire technology vouchsafed by a hierarchy of gods...

"Later, in monotheistic, Newtonian times, the universe was deemed to be operating like clockwork – running in accordance with a set of mathematical principles created by an omnipotent God, and we saw ourselves as biological mechanisms, as souls inhabiting organic 'automata' – reminiscent of the clockwork display pieces that were, at the time, the popular hi-tech toys of the aristocracy.

"Similarly, as we advanced through the age of chemistry and physics, the body was seen as a virtual laboratory of interactive chemicals – catalyctic, caustic, explosive, and it happened to be the era of violent societal change, of revolution, wars and imperial conquest. Then we move forward into the age of quantum mechanics and the computer, our perception of our existence changing yet again – until today we are electrochemical organisms, our brains glorified organic computers – and the general view is that we are some kind of bizarre accident, with no Creator God... But of course, no one can yet explain consciousness and we have no meaningful concept… until we create computers with self-awareness, maybe one day soon. At that point, our comprehension of ourselves will change yet again.

"Anthropologists are able to observe and confirm this phenomenon through the study of tribal peoples today, those with little technological advancement of their own, or no contact with our techno-world. They still base their existence on a hierarchy of gods, demons and ancestors, all of whom have to be placated – for fertility, a rich harvest, a successful hunt and good health. No different to how early Homo sapiens behaved worldwide. And so, from this premise, it is easy to see that Alien Abduction and the medieval concept of the Devil 'taking your soul' are not that far apart; they are exactly the same mythological concept, merely modified, or characterised, by current technological advancement; an admix of the sensibilities extant at the time and human imagination.

"Yes, not so far apart. Ah, we are such strange creatures; we have evolved from simple organisms, through dinosaurs and apes to being a sentient, high-tech species, and yet we are basically unchanged in essence. Think analogously of a horse and cart and a Bugatti Veyron… the latter is a technological marvel in terms of power, speed and efficiency compared to its forerunners, and yet, in principle, it's still a horse, the power source, pulling a cart. And, of course, it's argued that with all the hours we put in earning the money to pay for and maintain our cars, despite individually driving, say, ten thousand miles a year, we still only each achieve an average speed of 5 miles per hour, just like a horse and cart…

"But, I digress – back to Alien Abduction, or the Devil taking your soul, depending on which century you live in.

"Every culture, worldwide since language developed and stories were told, has legends of 'soul possession' woven into the fabric of their folklore – from earliest man, through all civilisations, up to the present day. We must, therefore, ask ourselves; are we hard wired to interpret that which we do not understand in such a way, even today, despite our scientific and psychological knowledge? Or, on the other hand, is there an element of truth therein?

"Well, I believe the latter, and I'd like to tell you why…

"Newton's Third Law states that 'for every action, there is an opposite and equal reaction'. Without that physical phenomenon, we wouldn't be able to walk, hit a ball with a bat, fly off to Majorca for our holidays, or swim while we're there. It is an undisputed physical fact.

Please pay attention, young man. You can chat to your girlfriend later.

"Now, as I was saying, Newton's Third Law... what if we were to apply this physical law to something as abstract as human evolution? If we do, something most peculiar arises – a direct correlation throughout history in which every human group action for 'good' is opposed by an opposite and equal reaction for 'bad'. By 'good' here I mean our evolutionary growth, from animal to human; our pushing the boundaries of scientific knowledge, our striving to become more sentient through learning and creativity, through becoming Individuated (in psychological terms) or becoming one with one's Maker (in religious terminology), as well as our innate desire for social justice and an equitable society. Civilisation, in a word. And by 'bad' I mean simply the power of entropy – the constant winding down, or spending, of energy throughout the Universe – hot to cold, light to dark, positive to negative, life to death.

"To my mind, and for the purposes of this lecture, that's where 'the Devil' concept enters into folklore worldwide, dressed up according to current belief systems, learning and language and the sensibilities of the age – its Zeitgeist. And, of course, as I've stated before, it's all intrinsically wrapped up with the technology available at the time...

"I'll now give you some examples of this 'war' from recent history. Once the power of Christianity had become established, there followed the Dark Ages – a period of ignorance and repression created by an all-powerful church that preached Christ's message, but acted in a completely opposite way.

"Then, as scientific breakthroughs began to enrich our lives, social cohesion started to fail on a hitherto unknown scale as the rich landowners got richer and the poor got poorer still, losing even their birthright as they were forced to move in droves from the countryside they knew into the foul towns of the Industrial Revolution. And, speaking of revolutions... take a sideways glance at the French and Russian Revolutions – both attempts to redress the balance, to create just and equitable societies – and what followed each, despite two hundred years between them? The Terror!

'Hands down, please. I'll take questions at the end of my lecture... Thank you. Now, where was I? Ah, yes. Let's take another random example – The Pilgrim Fathers and the New World... this advancement culminated in the Declaration of Independence. How does it go? 'We hold these truths to be self-evident, that all men are created equal, that they are endowed by their Creator with certain unalienable Rights, that among these are Life, Liberty and the pursuit of Happiness.' Oh, admirable thoughts, indeed, yet it took how long after they were uttered to abolish slavery? To allow women the vote? And even today, racism is still rife in that topsy-turvy land... a country that can reach the moon, yet still condones torture and allows the death penalty.

"At the turn of the twentieth century, great minds – amongst them Freud and Einstein – began to unravel the mysteries of the human psyche and the universe; great strides were made in the arts, the sciences and in every field. Following this surge forward came the First World War – the ruling families of old settling past scores using the proletariat as their weapon of mass destruction. The contrived peace that followed merely sowed the seeds for the next world conflict and the subsequent creation of atomic weapons and after, the debilitating Cold War.

"And now, we have moved into the age of the internet, an evolutionary move to bring mankind together as one global family... but, the entropy Devil is reacting against this force for good, for freedom, for common humanity, turning it into a tool of repression, a way of keeping tabs on us all by our so-called governments and facilitating the near collapse of our banking systems, from which, the result is, as ever, only the poor suffer...

"Now, I can almost hear you thinking 'Yeah, this is all very well on a world scale, but what about those Alien Abduction claims by individuals?' Well, I'm sure you're all aware of the concepts of microcosm in macrocosm and 'as above, so below'. I began to notice the phenomenon on an individual human scale when I was very young, but of course had no way of understanding what was happening to me then.

"It starts with small things... you try to help a friend in trouble and then they turn on you. You are generous with your sweets and somehow you lose the lot. Later, you fall for a girl, and you both profess undying love – later, she betrays you with your best friend; you get a job, work hard and are made redundant, or someone steals your research ideas... Slowly, inexorably as good is met with bad throughout an individual's life, the doubts and self-centredness creep in; the lack of trust, the closing the self off to other people, the refusing to come to anothers aid and so on, until the soul, the innermost self, is literally 'possessed' by a very different force than that which it started out with... It doesn't take much of a leap of the imagination for this to manifest psychotically as an Alien Abduction illusion-delusion; our mental institutions are full of schizophrenics and manic depressives, all of whom have experienced to the nth degree the backlash of the bad against their good, have experienced as reality the Devil taking their soul...

"Will you people who've just entered quickly find a seat, please. Ah! Not students, I see, but two of the Devil's henchmen in white coats...You see how it works? Just as I am attempting to enlighten you, to increase your understanding for your own good, the bad is countering with an equal and opposite force, disrupting my lecture, no doubt about to forcibly remove me..."

"Now come on, Nigel. Get down from that table..."

"Begone, I say!"

"Nigel... Get down – now..."

"Professor Braithwaite to you..."

"C'mon, now; down you come..."

"Unhand me, you minions of Beelzebub!"

"You know we've told you over and over you mustn't frighten the other patients with your crazy ideas... It's time for your medication, and then, when you're calm, we'll tuck you up for the night in your nice warm bed..."

20
LIFE CYCLES

E-RUNES FROM THE MINISTER FOR THE DEPARTMENT OF SCIENCE & TECHNOLOGY: 26 TH JULY, 2133
INTERNAL BRIEFING/UPDATE PAPER: PRIME MINISTER'S EYES ONLY

Dear Paul,

As you may be aware, it has long been established that everything in the universe is created from a single, particulate energy – not only everyday materiality, but also thought and the whole range of emotions. Each of these latter manifestations has been identified by their sub-atomic particulate structure and subsequently documented by the (classified) Psycho-Ops Group set up under the aegis of this department with your full support.

Recently, the group has identified the 'quintessence quotient' (aka 'soul') in a volunteer (a 74 year old former scientist and terminally ill cancer patient).

This group of particles has been isolated and rigged with the latest nanotech tracking and recording devices prior to the volunteer's death.

The following is a transcript of the movement data received after the event.

Only the four scientists involved in the experiment, myself and now you, are party to this information. We leave it to your discretion whether or not to consult with the Cabinet and to go public, or for the experiment to remain classified for the time being. Exciting times, what? Yours as ever,

Bill (Minister for Science and Technology)

Data Transcript Attachment:

The volunteer's body ceased functioning at 0113 hours. There was no apparent comprehension of the event by the quintessence; no identifiable record of pain or trauma, no upwelling of fear, panic or joy; just a neutral acceptance, as though this were normal, expected.

Neither was there awareness of the personality and life being left; there were no regrets, sadness, or sense of 'goodbye'; and no record of remembrance of the volunteer's family and friends etc.

There was no sense of time or place; however, lingering traces of corporality allowed the illusion of events happening sequentially. It is important to note that 'he' was no longer a male personality, but a neutral entity that we shall label 'Self'.

A veiled opening appeared ahead, muted light beyond, and Self passed through and for the first time became aware of the presence of other 'Selfs', with whom there was both connectivity and separation.

Contact with the other Selfs aroused an all-encompassing sensation – something immediately identifiable from earlier experiments as the bond underpinning the sense of family – a benign and all-forgiving love.

The group of selves continued forward momentum, eventually arriving as one in a great hall of light.

Here, the sensations of love intensified, as all traces of past-life fell away and understanding and recognition seemed to 'blossom', recorded as a huge surge of data input.

A group calling themselves 'The Ancients' manifested and communicated with the singularity of Selves. We are under the impression that The Ancients were fully aware of our experiment and augmented the transmissions for our benefit and, accordingly, we wre able to record their communication with the singularity.

"Welcome back. After a period of rest and relaxation, you will be returning as individuals again. But first, you will be reminded of the basic error you each made during your recent incarnations – the creation of a deeply flawed life-guide based solely on your parents' behaviour within your family unit. We shall then analyse together the individual misjudgements made, and how you can use your experience to avoid making the same mistakes again. Then, in consultation, we will choose a new venue for your next session.'

The Ancients then addressed our subject directly: 'Although you did well in your first life, attempting to be just, working hard and contributing to your society, the essence of your basic error in your case was to make a decision that meant you would never reach your full potential, despite the set of refined talents you were given. When a sibling was born into your family group, your burgeoning ego adopted the pose that your parents must think you were not enough, that you were somehow flawed. As you grew, instead of casting the erroneous guide aside, you attempted to edit reality to make it correspond with your 'not enough' beliefs. You did this collusively with the wife you married the friends you attracted and were attracted to, even the work you undertook. The false scenario created resulted in an ocean of anger, dissatisfaction, anxiety and guilt, continuously feeding your ego in a closed loop system.

'All human frailties – feeling affronted, anxious, cocksure, righteous and so on – stem from the ego. Ego rules whenever you feel arrogant or inferior, praised or criticised, over-happy or over-sad. And when ego rules, disconnectivity follows. I feel better than you, or I am less than you; we are right, they are wrong, or vice versa.

'To live without ego is essential if one wishes to remain an authentic self. For, if you act only from the authentic self, treating others only as you would be treated, how is it possible to harm another...?

'When you return to next-life, remember; you do not need to be more, or less, than you are. Celebrate your uniqueness, develop your talents. Your authentic self is as complete as possible...'

* * *

The new baby lies in her cot, recently fed and changed and now enjoying kicking her legs, aware only of being alive.

Meanwhile, the embedded nanotechs continue to record and transmit...

21

LE PEINTRE DE LA VIE MODERNE

'COME IN PLEASE, take a seat. You are...?'

'Justin Delcourt.'

'Ah, yes. It says in your CV that you studied painting, got your degree and are now working for your Doctorate.

'That's right.'

'Why the switch to the world of academia?'

'I felt I had nothing original to say as a painter – I could probably make a living forging any artist's work, but that's illegal, of course. And anyway, the history of art has more appeal now...'

'And your thesis is on "Le group de Picasso, Paris, 1906 –1914"?'

'Yes. I chose that era because I wanted to study the greats – not only Picasso, but other artists such as Rousseau, Daunier, Utrillo, Braque, Juan Gris, Matisse and Modigliani; and writers like Apollinaire, Alfred Jarry, Gertrude Stein and Jean Cocteau. Paris at the turn of the twentieth century was one of the most seminal, intellectually creative cultural enclaves ever – and all at a time of great change – Freud, science, transport, communications...'

'The Birth of Modernism, eh? I see you are bilingual?'

'I am. My mother was French, my father English, but I never knew him. My mother and I spent our time in both France and England.'

'Good. Well, I think this would be an ideal framework for an experimental module to include in our work – and you are an ideal candidate. You've passed the medical, you're very fit, both physically and mentally. Perfect! So, if you care to follow me, I'll show you round the facility and explain a little more.'

'This is the "bedroom" as we call it. It cost the taxpayer a few billion pounds. This where you'll live attached to the computer complex – you'll be gone for about a week, which is about two and a half years in virtual time. During the week, you'll be monitored physically and mentally and fed and watered – a bit like a coma patient. We'll be constantly uploading into the system all the sensory perceptions you'll need. And during the sleep, we'll be recording and assessing all your neural activity – reading your thoughts, in other words. When you enter the field at first, it'll take some getting used to. It will seem as real as normal life, but as in a dream, you will still have a conscious overview. This will enable you to have a degree of control so you'll be able to write down observational comments, which we'll also record through your brain activity. We'll need time to program and set up the data-bank parameters, and to feed in all the known data of your era, so, we'd expect you to report in this time next week. Any questions?'

'Yes. When do I get paid?'

* * *

I was in a coma alright – for about six months, so I'm told. I was only supposed to be 'out' for a week, but they couldn't revive me until a few days ago. They said it had never happened before, that I was unique and it was probably because I'm an artist and art historian and was too intensely identified with my era; and they'd like to keep me in for observation for a while, just in case. I guess they're worried I might file a lawsuit…

The session was so realistic. It truly seemed as though I was sitting in a room I'd rented in the Bateau Lavoir – just across from Picasso's studio. Max Jacob called the ramshackle bunch of wooden buildings in Monmartre 'Le Bateau Lavoir' after the laundry boats on the Seine, because they too creaked and groaned in the winter storms.

Before entering the experiment, they gave me a sturdy avatar so I could earn money labouring until I got established as an artist. The arduous, back-breaking work, the perspiration and aching muscles were just as vivid as in real life.

Time passed as real time, so I had to sleep and eat and go to the loo and wash and shave, negotiate, buy food – just like real life.

The genius is, although it seems like real time, a couple of months there would only be a day in reality. And this was my 'problem' – I was out for six months, the equivalent of roughly 60 years – a painter's working lifetime.

I asked how they did that trick with time and they said that in reality, everything happens more or less simultaneously, but it's all interpreted by a part of the brain that measures time and we some-how merge all the sensory input to give our world the appearance of linear, sequential time passing. And normally, we only fall out of the illusion when we're in a lower state of consciousness, such as when asleep and dreaming, or when we're really enjoying some-thing or bored. And of course, we all know that stimulating precise neural-networks in the brain can reprise anything it has previously experienced – including emotions, hot or cold, the taste of food, the wind on the skin, right through to a full blown orgasm – and with Picasso's crowd, I had plenty of them.

So, I drank what tasted like real coffee, ate what seemed like genuine baguettes, smoked French cigarettes and listened to apparently real-life Parisienne sounds coming through the open window (along with authentic smells!).

They can even recall for you all conversations and anything written – it's all electrical impulses and digitised stuff going on in there, after all.

Here are some of the early days' jottings they recorded for me:

"Right now, I'm sitting at a desk having breakfast and writing up my notes. I've been here three months according to the calendar, and now I have enough money, I'm finally ready to meet my heroes.

"The most difficult part is absorbing the Zeitgeist; I know my art history of this period like the back of my hand, and I've been reading newspapers and magazines and going to theatres and music halls non-stop, but it's difficult to tune in, despite being bilingual – but I've managed to pick up the local argot and can pass for real.

"I also have to get used to the sexual and social mores; women look so strange to me in early 20th century dress, and there's a really powerful class system based on money and position – I find it difficult to be off-hand with waiters, for example. And everybody's pretty lax about personal hygiene... Hopefully, any faux-pas I make will be put down to my being English, which I'll be presenting myself as...

Later: "Well that went well. I walked up to Picasso's group dining in the Le Chat Noir and said, with a bow, 'Pardon, Messieurs, je cherche Pablo Picasso, l'artiste...'

"Picasso is shorter than I expected, but very compact, well built, strong and bullish looking. He's swarthy complexioned and has thick, black hair, with a fringe falling across his forehead. As I remembered from old silver colloid photos of him when young, he has a large nose and full mouth and the eyes are huge, intense, boring into you.

"I introduced myself using my real name; Picasso also uses his mother's maiden name, realising early on, perhaps, that his family name, Riz, didn't have quite the correct ring for a world-shattering artist. I told them I was an English painter, come to live, work and study in Paris and had rented a studio in le Bateau Lavoir, feigning surprise when Picasso said, 'Ah, so we are neighbours...'

"Then I told them that my main influence was Cézanne and slipped in his maxim about treating nature as the cube, the cylinder and the cone, and was immediately accepted, and an in-depth conversation kicked off, my having to be very careful with mid-21st century vernacular, and to hold back on my knowledge of the future.

"Picasso is very quick on the uptake – and very intelligent, yet comes across as unsophisticated as a schoolboy, in some ways (he's only 25). He's also moody and mercurial, obviously the group leader, and I wouldn't like to upset him too much (he enjoys boxing in his spare time).

"If you know anything about art, you'll know that Picasso's 1907 painting, 'Les Demoiselles D'Avignon' – five prostitutes in an almost dimensionless space, staring dispassionately out at the viewer with mask-like faces – was the seminal masterpiece of the 20th century. It was truly shocking in its day – Picasso turned it to the wall of his studio and didn't exhibit it for some years, and even his avant-garde, artist friends didn't understand it. But it changed the direction of western art for ever.

"My idea for the experiment was to do it all before Picasso and to become the star of the group – no more 'Le group de Picasso', but 'Le group de Delcourt'. Truth is, I've taken a dislike to him. He may well have set a process in motion that changed the way we see and experience art in my world today (or should that be tomorrow?), but he's arrogant and selfish and I wouldn't trust him an inch. So, in my virtual life as a painter, I'm going to do it bigger and better than he did, and before him. And I can because I'm informed by what he achieved. How's that for irony?"

More of my notes: 'Pablo! Bienvenue! Rentres...'

Picasso visited my studio last night. He's obviously intrigued, and maybe feels threatened by me; he wants to sound me out, I guess; get to know his enemy (God, he's so competitive, jealously guards his leadership of the group).

He asked me what I was working on, so I showed him my sketches for my version of Les Demoiselles. Of course, I'd already seen and studied and absorbed the sketches he hasn't even done yet, so he was pretty flabbergasted – especially as I'd given them a slightly more modern treatment.

'What are you trying to achieve?' he quizzes me.

'Have you read Baudelaire's essay "Le Peintre de la Vie Moderne"?'

'I know of it… He was referring to the work of Guys…'

'Precisely, The man who drew the fashionable promenading and scenes from the brothel. And you know Manet's "Olympia" – the courtesan staring dispassionately and amorally out at the viewer with that '"I know what you men want" look? That is the effect I seek.'

'Oui, oui - ça je comprends. Mais les visages. Ils sont grotesques, non?'

'My influences come from African sculpture. Have you been to La Trocadéro?' I ask him, again pre-empting his epiphany of a visit, when he spent the whole day totally immersed in the mask displays, changing his style completely.

'The masks represent raw emotion, without artifice. Do you know the writings of Sigmund Freud, a German neurologist? You should read him, he is doing great work exploring what he terms 'the subconscious'… It has led me to believe our conservative values of realism are false, our values and manners mere masks to hide our true, animal natures. We must get to the underlying reality, and we can only do that through a symbolic art. There should be no more perspective, no more static, fixed-viewpoint representation of the human form by techniques and painterly artifice – and we must reject classical attitudes and tradition – plus this certainty of the old Enlightenment thinking. And we must abandon the concept of the existence of a compassionate, all-powerful Creator God. We are self-conscious animals, driven by our urges, mere biological machines… Art from now on will become the result of the viewer viewing an object – I eventually see an art where the materials and process used are more important than any narrative…'

Picasso is staring at me, awestruck, I sense.

'We must make it new!' I emphasise, quoting something Ezra Pound will write in thirty years time. We continue discussing this for some time, until Picasso looks at his watch. and announces, 'Come, let us visit Madame Bouverie's before supper…'

* * *

Around this time, the experimenters lost me. No more data was recorded. I was in limbo.

'We were pretty worried,' they admitted. 'But we kept you alive and healthy. And then we got you back.'

I have no recall of what happened after my brothel visit, no sense of time passing. It just seemed like a normal night's deep and dreamless sleep. The next thing I knew was waking up in a very bright room, feeling fully awake and very, very hungry.

* * *

When I finally left the hospital, even though all tests came up as positive or negative as they should be, I knew something wasn't quite right.

Zooming home in the jetaxi, staring out the window, nothing looked totally familiar any more. The logos, the hoardings, the buildings all looked peculiar, out of kilter, the colours wrong, the language slightly odd, as though a literal translation from a foreign tongue. I shrugged it off as probably just the result of a six months coma and being somewhat disoriented.

Once settled in my apartment and my house computer up and running, I settled down to work. Again, the imagery looked strange, foreign... Was there something the doctors had missed? Something not quite right with my brain? The thought was accompanied with a trill of anxiety.

'Thesis; Picasso,' I told the computer.

Instead of the usual pages of notes, just a paragraph: 'Picasso: 1889 – 1910. Minor Spanish painter known for the Blue and Pink series of paintings. Committed suicide in Paris 1910.'

'What the...?' On a hunch, I suggested, 'Delcourt'.

'The greatest artist of the twentieth century... his master piece 'Les Demoiselles D'Avignon' changed the direction of western art... the father of the modernism... little is known of the early life of this French artist, but it is believed he was born in England... international reputation... awarded the Nobel Peace Prize for his anti-war protest painting 'London Blitz'... his name is a byword for 'modern art'... he died at the age of 93 in Paris...'

Page after page about my alter ego. I looked over at my bookshelves. Instead of 'Picasso', 'Delcourt' leapt from spine after spine...

How had this happened? Had the experiment somehow tampered with the fabric of reality? Had I slipped into a parallel universe?

And then it dawned...

'Oh, *merde*! I'm not back yet; I'm still in the fuckin' experiment...'

22

FRAGMENT

AS THE LAST sentient being alive in this particular universal manifestation, I feel it is incumbent upon me, purely for posterity's sake, to record as much of my metaphysical savoir faire as possible in the hope that it might be useful to a future entity in another universe some day.

First, a little background information. I am currently heading out into space in one of our technological marvels at a velocity approaching the speed of light, simply to gain a little more time before our red giant of a star engulfs my home planet in approximately 2.35 orbits time – and me and my craft shortly after.

At the very last moment, as I begin to be re-absorbed, I shall beam this information into the empty bubble that was once our universe (all other stars having burnt out) trusting that this message will survive in some format or other. After all, no thing is ever lost, its constituent parts merely transform into some thing else, eventually.

Some two million orbits after this all happens, our local Red Giant will collapse, becoming a neutron star. It will then quickly use itself up, explode, become a supernova and finally disappear into a black hole of its own making.

What remains of the whole ex-universe will then gradually entropy to a soup of positive and negative particles. These will then cancel each other out, become energy-less and time and space will cease to exist at this location as it all shrinks back into the All-That-Is.

That is the way all universes end. The reverse process is how they begin, but I'm getting ahead of myself.

In a sense, I'm recording this information for an imaginary being, let's say one living on a planet some hundred million miles from an average star which is about half way through its ten billion years' life cycle in any one of any of the infinite number of universes to follow.

Well, my naïve young friend, your civilisation is probably at the stage where you are searching for 'alien life'out there in the ether, while still believing there is an Omnipotent Creator God.

The God you imagine is, most probably, some form of loving, transcendent, artistic, mathematical genius, who has determined a set of complex formulae, summoned enormous amounts of energy and willed "Let there be light!' and created your universe. And I wonder if you hold the theory, like so many young and inexperienced, yet extraordinarily self-regarding, civilisations before, that He has somehow created you 'in His own image'?

The following may come as a surprise. There is no 'God', but there are an infinite number of 'gods'.

The gods are 'All-that-Is'. They were not created, they simply exist (and invented 'creativity', so don't bother to ask, 'Who created them?'). They are eternal in that they live outside of 'time' (they create that, too). They are as one, but individual. They have no beginning and no end; there is no inside or outside of them; they do not take up space, they are not anywhere, but everywhere.

I could never describe them to you, no more than the ship I am in could describe me. But I can conjure up an analogy.

They are as a sponge – phylum Porifer – the most primitive of all living entities. Within their eternal existence they create the bubbles of space into which they, as individuals, divert energy to create a universe filled with stars and planets and all their various inter-related life forms.

These gods are a mixed bunch. Some are caring, some callous, a few insane; there are even those jealous of others' creations and will sabotage them if they can; many are petty-minded, or angry, slapdash, others perfectionists. But, the one thing they share is total amorality.

They have 'personalities', yet are, of course, not persons, per se. They are simply eternal beings, outside of time, outside of space, yet inside and outside of their creations.

The reason they bother to make universes is mainly because they know nothing else, but they do it for a kind of pleasure as well. But, of course, their pleasures, their qualia, differ. The sentimentalists among them do it for the beauty of a moon rising in a late autumn sky; the smell of fresh bread; the sound of the sea breaking on a shore. Some enjoy voyeuristic sex, some the softness of a newborn's skin; others enjoy cruelty, lapping up the death throes of prey hunted down by predators; there are even those who enjoy the spectacle of total warfare, natural disasters, and exstinction of species – and those who revel in the screams of the tortured.

At this point, I can almost hear you asking what happens to us when we die? This is a tricky one to explain. Most of 'you', your constituent particles, your physicality, goes back into the melting pot and is transformed back into raw energy and will be used over and again. That includes all your memories, thoughts, experiences – everything, all of which is merely energy, but organised in appropriate, fitness-for-purpose formats.

However, as a sentient being, you owe your consciousness to the god directly responsible for your universe. The awareness you have been given is part of your creator-god's, it is not your own and it will be subsumed when your allotted lifespan is up.

As you return, this will appear, at first, as though you are ascending, or transcending, into a higher realm. This may seem like the 'heaven' prophesied in your sacred books. But the joy experienced will soon pall when you are reabsorbed into the banality of a god's consciousness of its own existence. The gods are forced to work ceaselessly as they attempt to outdo one another with the cleverness of their creations. They are, therefore, overworked, stressed out, bored and basically very unhappy.

And you will, of course, now you are one of them again, re-experience all the fears, worries, anxieties, difficulties you experienced in your existence as a created being, but this time on an unimaginably enormous scale.

However, after a while, you will settle in to the routine of a god's hum-drum life and perhaps be part of that nostalgic yearning for something better that is the background hum to their eternal existence.

There's another rather important concept you need to understand (I'm presuming that you are at the stage where you are actually blinded by your own science, that you are already 'knowledge bound' and unable, therefore to see what is there before your eyes). Although the gods have been creating universes for an eternity and have the technique off pat, at the sub-atomic level they have still difficulty converting their reality into something their created beings can tolerate, so they are forced to inject a 'certainty principle'. In their realm, all possibilities exist simultaneously, whereas in ours, certainty rules out all other possibilities at the moment of choice. This allows us the illusion of time moving sequentially as each morning we awake, we immediately reaffirm all the other choices we have ever made, thus stabilising our sense of self. We quite happily then believe we are this, or that – an entity with a set lifespan, gender, personality and so on.

Again, I hear you questioning how my species are party to this information. The answer is simply that our home god decided, in his wisdom, to reveal all. Now, it is possible that these revelations are a sick joke and are quite meaningless...

(This fragment, picked up by the Lovell radio telescope at Jodrell Bank, ends here. We continue to search for the rest of the transmission.)

23
REMINDER

MEMO TO MYSELF:

When you read this you will still be unaware of your true nature. You will, no doubt, still be thinking that you are an individual living on a planet circling a sun in a galaxy – one of billions comprising a Universe.

You may think that this Universe happened by chance and you were born, will live and then die and that's all there is to it. Or you may believe that there is an Absolute Being who created and sustains the Universe with His power and that you have an eternal soul and that, if morally good, it will reside in paradise forever after you die; or again, you may hold that the Universe created itself and you are merely one of its myriad temporary manifestations and will eventually merge back into it again until your next appearance as, say, a butterfly, a zebra, or a great king.

Comforting as these thoughts may be, nothing could be further from the truth.

What I am about to tell you, or rather remind you of, may come as a shock at first, but you'll get used to it, as you and I always do.

Yes, you and I are one and the same, my friend. There is only you, as there was/is only me. You and I create our life, our reality – no one or no thing else exists.

We, you and I, make it all up. Everything. Our life, our world – and what ever happens around us.

We, me, you, are pure, eternal existence. Always were always are and always will be.

And I, you, we, get lonely and bored.

So you and I create a virtual world around us. Nothing exists but as you and I will it, and want it, and make it.

Me and you. We write the play and act it out with ourself at the centre, surrounded by an imaginary cast of players. You stub your toe? It's in the script. Your girlfriend leaves you for another man? You include them both in the *Dramatis Personae*, write the scene for them, then direct the action, making sure there's a juicy role for yourself, of course. (I'm afraid we are a little 'me-me-me'.)

An earthquake on the other side of the world? You conjure the *mise en scene*, design and build the scenery and then stage the event.

People around you die? You write them out.

You make a million, or you're a pauper; you live a long and happy life and pass away in your sleep; or experience a painful, lingering death – whatever the outcome, you invent the plot, write the storyline.

And when you pull down the final curtain, when you 'die', everything disappears, does it not? The play ends, the make-up and the costumes come off, the players go home, the scenery is struck and the audience leaves the theatre.

All of it is you... and me.

Then you begin to write another spectacular – something completely different this time; perhaps, as the star of the show (always, always), you're a Mexican prostitute, or a Martian surgeon, a Jovian graphic designer, or a Venusian ballerina...

And so it goes on, always has and always will, for creativity is endless, you are endless. You can't die – death is something you and I invented to add a bit of spice...

Are you remembering yet? Is it all coming back? Bummer, eh?

This reminder (artfully delivered, what, in this book of sci-fi shorts you're reading) is designed to make sure I/you/we don't get stuck in this current production.

A bit of a wake up call if you like.

So, don't forget to write another reminder, a prompt, and make sure you put it somewhere you will find it, or it will be found, during my/your/our next production.

Yours, as ever,

Me, myself and I.

PS: Do try and come up with something a little more post-modern next time. I'm getting bored with universes.

24

BLIND DATE

'OKAY! FIRST QUESTION. Why should I pick you? That goes to number one.'

'Hallo, Adam. Well, you should pick me because I'm fresh, fruity and fully matured; my body is well proportioned, my flesh firm, crisp and juicy, my skin very smooth and rosy – and I smell as nice as I look. I'm also clean and have no diseases – and I know, if you bite me, you're sure to get both our juices flowing.'

(*Laughter*.) 'Sounds good. What else are you offering?'

'Well, Adam, I'm offering you something I know you want in your innermost depths. The chance to evolve, to become master of your own destiny rather than remaining as a created puppet.

'I know everything in the Garden seems to be coming up roses, right now, but let's take a look at the reality. On the surface, it looks as though you have everything you need, that Eden is a paradise; but, you can only eat what falls into your lap, so to speak. You can't plan or plant or harvest and store, because you don't know how to make tools, so thanks to the seasons, for three quarters of the year you go hungry. And you can't hunt because you don't know how to make weapons; neither can you raise livestock, because you don't know the first thing about farming. You're neither hunter nor gatherer – more of a hobo, really – except you daren't move away from the local water supply (which you're beginning to foul up, by the way, but what do you know of sanitation?).

'And what do you do at night apart from eat, make love and sleep? Because you haven't developed language, you have no literature, there's no entertainment, no books, nothing to talk about. Just the same old, thoughtless same-old, over and over. You're nothing more than a two-legged animal at the moment. And, yes, you do look odd without a belly button, but we'll overlook that for now...

'And as for science and technology, I bet you don't even know what they are...

'So, this is what I'm offering in a nutshell – the chance to develop your mind and to get down and dirty with this world, to get to grips with it and develop it to its maximum potential.

'Now, I know it won't be easy, Adam. The Old Man is going to be a bit miffed if you pick me, and he'll probably turn his back on you and cast you out – but you've got to see that as freedom, the chance to be your own man, to be somebody.

'Yes, it's going to be tough for millennia, but you will come through, you will evolve to a higher being and then you'll know all the travail was worth it.

'What I'm offering you, Adam, is knowledge. Knowledge of yourself, of this world, of creation.

'You have no past to speak of and a dead-end present, but I'm offering you a future.

'So, don't let me remain the forbidden fruit – pick me and let me be the apple of your eye...'

25
TIME AFTER TIME

THE BEDROOM WALLS are diamond-patterned by the full moon's icy light pouring through the window. Wide awake, lying on his side, Alan stares at the winking red colon separating the numbers two and forty-four on the alarm clock. When it begins to pulse in time with his heart-beat, he finds the sensation disturbing and turns over. His wife groans in her sleep, rolls onto her back and begins to snore a softly sonorous semi-tone lower than the droning fridge-freezer downstairs.

He knows sleep is impossible now and, feeling irritated, slips out of bed to gather his dressing gown from where it hangs wraith-like on the door.

Carrying a mug of tea into the sitting room, he stretches out on the sofa, picks up the remote and channel hops. After half an hour, tired of watching chat shows and Open University programmes with the sound so low he can hardly hear it, he switches off and creeps back upstairs to his study, where he checks e-mail, hastily turning down the volume as the chirpy dialling tone echoes through the sullen house.

'You have new mail' the screen tells him. A scattering of messages; three for wholesale Viagra, two get-rich-quick schemes, a cheap mortgage refinancing offer (for US residents only) and one headed 'Remember me?'. He opens it, intrigued, and reads:

> hi alan, if you remember birds, bob dylan, maryland road and snow, you might remember me too. anyway – just writing to see how you are etc don't know what to say in fact, been along time. what are you up to these days? married? kids? working? how's your mum?
> best wishes mitsuko :)

He sits stunned. Yes, he remembers... never a day goes by when he doesn't, along with an old, well-worn hurt...

Mitsuko. 1985. And birds. A surprising swell of nostalgia surges in his chest. They had only been going out together a few weeks that sunny, autumn day when he fell in love with her. She had been to the opticians to collect her first pair of glasses and they had met, as arranged, in the small park close to the college. She was nineteen at the time, an architecture student, he a year older and a year above her, studying at the same college…

He sees her again, walking towards him across the park wearing a short black skirt and tight, buff-coloured roll-necked jumper – willowy, long-legged and small-breasted.

– God, that face. Half Japanese; stunning almond eyes, sensuous lips, olive skin, tumultuous black hair…

She sat down on the bench beside him and sprang open a brand new glasses case. Placing the wire-framed spectacles on the bridge of her nose and gingerly pushing the side pieces over her ears, she turned to face him.

'What do you think?'

'Nice. Kind of sexy-intellectual.'

'Oh, please, no. They all thought I was such a swot at school.'

'Were you?'

'Not at all. It was only because I studied cello.' She looked around the park, attempting to accustom her eyes to the new sharpness of vision, then started to laugh.

– Her laugh. Like arpeggios cascading from middle C down to a plummy E…

A pang of yearning detonates in his chest exactly as it did that day.

'What's so funny?'

'The birds. I never really noticed them before. The way some walk and others hop. Why's that?'

He followed her gaze and saw a gaggle of birds squabbling over some abandoned sandwiches strewn on the path. It was true. The magpies and crows strutted self-importantly, their bodies rolling from side to side, heads jerking to-and-fro. The sparrows and starlings hopped, legs together, with precise little jumps, darting around the bigger birds as though powered by clockwork.

'They're so funny,' she laughed and he couldn't help but join in, seeing her so joyful, just being with her, drowning in her honeyed atmosphere.

– Christ, I was so alive then. In love, no worries, no responsibilities. Just sheer, happiness… until she…

He recalls the first time they made love. She lived with her family, a half hour train commute from college. He had visited, they'd gone out for a drink and, because he had missed the last train home, her parents naively offered him the sofa. She shook him awake in the middle of the night. It was humid, a storm was brewing, distant lightning, rumbling thunder.

He rocks on his seat, eyes closed, engulfed in a heavy-sweet yearning.

– *Her skin was so soft. And she smelled and tasted of.... What was it? Something so exotic, so Eastern, so spicy. And we came together that first time, stuffing fingers into our mouths to stifle our cries. And after, we lay there, talking in whispers until the dawn crept in and we made love one more time and she went back to her room...*

Feeling giddily regenerated and very awake, he compiles a reply.

Hi Mitsuko
It was such a pleasure to get your e-mail just now and it brought back so many fond memories.
I will give you an update of what's been happening to me over the last 35-odd years (yes, that long!) since we last met, on the proviso that you do the same and reply to me with all your news.Things like did you get married to that aristo geezer? Do you have children? What do you do for work and fun? Where are you living? More importantly, perhaps, what do you think of the world and life so far?
As for me, well, it's been happy, sad, fun, boring exhilarating, gruelling, beyond my wildest dreams, fulfilling, disappointing... you name it.
I'm a partner in a small architectural practice (nothing exciting - mostly civic stuff and extensions). For fun, I play guitar (still) in a sixties cover band. We play a gig most weeks, sometimes two or three and I really enjoy it. In many ways, I realise that this is what I'd love to have done. But maybe things aren't as good as you think when you do them professionally. Grass, greener and fences spring to mind.
On the personal front, I'm married to Ann and have been for twenty years. She's a teacher. Are we happy? We get along OK. Comfortable, I suppose. We have three daughters, all at Uni now, and none of them with kids yet, thank God (don't wanna be a grandfather just yet). You asked after my Mum... she's 85 now (my Dad died 10 years ago) and good apart from needing new knees which she'll get in a month's time... well, metal ones.
I could go on and on but don't want to bore you. I would really love to know what you've been up to so please e-mail back soon.
Your old friend Alan (Delaney) x

He spends time re-reading and crafting his response. Satisfied it says what he wants – expressing keenness without being too gushy, and that it bears no trace of recrimination – he clicks 'send'.

Dawn is breaking and the cloudless sky graduates from the palest lemon yellow to navy blue. He opens the window and breaths the cold air. He feels excited, expectant; happy for the first time in a long time.

That evening, after a dreamy day at work, unable to concentrate, he rushes home early, nervously anticipating her reply.

> hi alan, so glad you answered. yes, i have lots of fond memories too. often wondered what became of you. yes, I did marry the prince and went to live in japan (had no choice, did i?) but it did-n't work out (he was violent, among other things) and i came back to england after seven years. we had two children but he has cus-tody of them. then I got married again to a brit, had two more children but that was a disaster too, but my kids are fine. there was another one... but that didn't work out either. you probably think i'm terrible... but I'm not. just unlucky in love, i suppose. now I live in bristol on my own and work for various charities. i pass my time studying chinese and russian (never did finish my architecture course). could we meet sometime? i have something I want to ask you.
> mitsuko

Feeling elated he conjures scenarios of her on his arm, accompany-ing him to gigs; breakfasting together; sitting taking coffee in the sun somewhere in Europe – Italy probably; making passionate love in hotel rooms; his girl again.

    – She really was the original new woman in those days. Wanted to try everything. Every position, anywhere, anytime. And because she always knew she was destined to marry that Japanese prince, she expected me to treat the relationship as a bit of no-commitment fun, too. Unfortunately for me, I fell in love with her...

He touches again on the pain of the break up – and his subsequent breakdown. It is like biting on a rotten tooth.

> Dear Mitsuko
> Yes, let's meet. We've a lot of catching up to do. By chance, I'm coming to Bristol next Tuesday to see a client. Could we have tea late afternoon? Do you know the café in the Arnolfini Centre?

We could meet there about 4pm. I enclose a picture so you'll recognise me. Send me one if you can and hope you can make it.
Lots of love
Alan xxx

They do have clients near Bristol and it'll be easy to contrive a convincing reason to visit. Downstairs, he hunts through the family photo albums, strewing them across the floor, but can only find a photo he likes from about fifteen years ago. It is a shot of him playing in a band and he thinks he looks a little like Rod Stewart. As he sits on the floor staring at it, drenched in nostalgia, his wife enters the room.

'I'm off to the gym. I've left supper by the microwave. Two minutes. What you looking for?'

'Erm, an old mate from school contacted me through Friends Reunited. Billy Cooper. Wanna send him a photo.'

'Right. Make sure he's not turned gay first. Gotta go. See you later. Don't forget to put the albums away. Bye.'

Upstairs, he attaches the scanned and retouched photo, then sends.

Every half-hour throughout the evening he accesses his e-mail, longing for a response, all the while experiencing flashbacks. That night at her parents house...

'...I want you in my bed. Come to my room in half an hour,' she whispered in his ear as they parted at the top of the stairs, while her parents fussed and tidied the kitchen before retiring for the night.

As they made love, a sharp knocking at the door.

'Mitsuko! Alan isn't in his room,' her father announced, controlled outrage in his voice.

'Quick, down the side,' she hissed, pushing him in panic.

As he slid into the space between the bed and the wall, he was aware of her getting up, going to the door, opening it a crack.

'He just went for a walk. He won't be long.'

'That's damned inconsiderate of him,' her father huffed. He was an army type, upright, colonial. He'd met and married Mitsuko's mother in Japan, then 'gone native', adopting Shintoism to satisfy her aristocratic parents. On occasions, he displayed the religious zeal of a convert, celebrating the *shichigosan* and *setsubun* festivals, praying to his ancestors – even keeping a shrine at home. Most of the time he tolerated, and rather enjoyed arguing with, Mitsuko's atheist college friends. After all, she *was* betrothed and he and his wife could trust her not to become damaged goods.

Alan was no threat at first – the arranged marriage deal into an aristocratic Japanese family had been struck and was to be consolidated as soon as she finished college. At that moment, standing at his daughter's bedroom door, made impotent by the clashing of suspicion, propriety and good manners, he either didn't see through her lie, or didn't want to.

– I remember stuffing the blanket into my mouth, trying not to laugh. It was so exciting, like being in a movie, living life to the edge...

It wasn't long after that he was banned from their house and she forbidden to see him any more. That's when their relationship became a trysting secret, heavily spiced with the risk of being caught out.

– God! Those eroticised, clandestine meetings; fabricated evening lectures, theatre visits with girlfriends, her parents the shared enemy...

And the sense of victory when she took digs near her college, but spent all her time at his place, virtually moving in.

– We were like star-crossed lovers. Romeo and Juliet, Eloise and Abelard. And I was crazy for her and that sense of magic she created around us. Heaven. Everything numinous. Nearly destroyed me when they took her away...

He realises the pain has never gone away, aware that he hates her for what she did to him. And yet...

Around ten o'clock her e-mail arrives. She will meet him next Tuesday, is looking forward to it. There is no picture, though. He types a confirming reply and goes urgently to bed, longing to be snuggled alone with his imagination and the reconjured memories.

For the rest of the week he lives in the virtual dream world of the infatuated schoolgirl, rehearsing conversations with her, wondering how it will be when they go to bed together again, convinced they will. He books a hotel room in advance and tells his wife and partners he has to stay over for more meetings. He decides he will ask Mitsuko to go away with him. The thought delivers a trill of anticipation.

– We could start a new life together. I've some money I've saved from gigs. Sod everything else. It'll work out...

On the drive to Bristol he feels as excited as a kid going to the seaside, as apprehensive as a teenager on a first date.

– I'm in love with her all over again. This is so totally crazy, so fucking gung ho, but it's what I want. I'm Lazarus back from the dead...

At the appointed time, he walks into the Arnolfini and approaches the almost deserted café area, heart pounding. He scans the tables and sees her. He knows it is her despite the shock of her aged appearance and fuller figure. He realises it had never occurred to him she might look different, older...

She sees him approaching, stands and half smiles. He waves and smiles back. As he moves towards her, he reels under the weight of... what is it? Disappointment? No, an oppressive sense of diminution coupled with a rising bitterness.

He sees she looks just like her mother did all those years ago.

– *She must've been a beauty in her time. Too young to see it then, I suppose...*

He suddenly remembers the night her parents came to the house, righteously enraged, banging on the door, catching them in their night clothes. *In delicto flagrante...*

– *They'd found out we were living together, came to take her away...*

There was a shouting match. He recalls her mother sobbing at him, 'One day you'll have daughters and you'll know what this is like. How could you? My daughter?' Her mother's tears flowed while her tight-lipped father packed Mitsuko's things – a man betrayed, more infuriated by his own gullibility than by his daughter's duplicity.

He remembers being paralysed, rigid with his own frustrated anger, because she became so docile; just went along with it, like it was inevitable, the time, mere fate. Then they drove away and she looked dispassionately out of the car's rear window. A shrug and a half-smile.

– *God, that hurt!*

And he never saw or heard from her again.

Closer now, he sees she still retains the essence of her former beauty, but the vibrancy and sexiness are somehow repressed, under wraps.

'Mitsuko...'

'Alan.' She seems pleased to see him. He leans forward to kiss her on the cheek. She pulls back and sits.

She refuses his offer of tea or coffee, and when he returns with his, they sit and reminisce about old college friends and tutors, and then about their lives, seeming to skirt around their own past relationship.

'God, I really was in love with you in those days,' Alan finally volunteered. 'I was shattered when they took you away. Had a bit of a breakdown in fact...'

'Alan, I know. I'm aware of that now, of how much I must have hurt you. Please, will you forgive me? Really, truly forgive? From the depths of your heart? It's very, very important to me, please...?'

Alan slumped back in his chair, rubbing his brow. He didn't expect this. His emotions are in turmoil, anger rising.

'Please, Alan. I cannot move on until you do. I'm begging you...'

'I have to go to the loo,' he says, standing. 'Back in a minute.'

In the gents he leans forward, hands on the wash basin, staring numbly into the mirror.

– My God! What an idiot! Look at me. Old man. Going grey, fat gut. All in my head. Did I really think I could get it all back?

And then a final, cathartic, crushing blow.

– She never loved me. Egoistic, self-serving, bitch...

– Listen to yourself. You've been a self-centred prat all your life...

'Will you ever do anything right?' he demands of his reflection, out loud, striking the basin with his palm for emphasis. A tear flows down his cheek.

– Yes... I can forgive. I must – got to be free of this...

A wave of good feeling neutralises his self-recrimination. Suddenly, he feels light again, as though taking off a heavy rucksack carried for miles. He splashes cold water over his face, dries off and walks back into the café...

* * *

"Yes, that's right. Mitsuko Ashley-Cooper, with a hyphen. Are you sure? No record at all? No Mitsuko anything?"

It is a week later and Alan is desperately trying to trace her She had disappeared when he returned from the café lavatory, and since then has not responded to any of his e-mails.

He had poured over hers in the hope of finding a clue – but found no address, no phone number. Apart from her name, knowing she lived in Bristol and studied languages, he had nothing to go on.

'Why did she walk off?' he asks himself. 'Just when I had forgiven her at last. We could have at least been friends...'

He returns to his Googled list of twenty Bristol language schools and clicks on the penultimate, proceeds to its contact page, writing down the telephone number and forlornly dialling.

"Yes, Mitsuko used to be a student here," the receptionist answers.

"Great! Do you have a current address or contact number for her, please?"

"Er, sorry, no... Oh dear. This is difficult. You obviously don't know... I'm afraid she's dead – car accident if I remember rightly...'

'What? When did this happen?' Alan blurted, incredulous.

'Oh, it must have been at least three years ago...'

26

THE TWO PANDORAS

IT WAS ABOUT five years into our marriage when my wife and I finally accepted that we'd never have children. My wife's tubes were apparently blocked, and in those days there were no reliable surgical procedures available, no test-tube babies as the popular press call them now; and, anyway, my sperm count was not what it should be. We talked about adoption, but it seemed such a long, protracted process with only ethnic minority or disabled children 'on offer' (how callous that sounds today – children as commodities). In that pre-PC era, we felt we couldn't cope with any social trauma that might result from such a strategy. So we developed our careers and had cats instead.

We got into a pattern of allowing each cat one litter before having it speyed, and of then keeping one female kitten. Many generations came and went over the years as road accidents culled the younger cats, disease and old age overtaking the eldest. Sometimes we'd have four cats, a great grandmother, granny, mother and a daughter, sometimes three. Then there was a time when we had only the one – a spinsterish daughter who somehow never became pregnant.

She was not a pretty cat, but tough and resourceful, and we called her Pandora – my wife plucking the name at random while holding the mewling kitten up to her smiling eyes.

Then one day, perhaps ten years later, Pandora didn't come in for her food, nor the day after, nor the next – she just disappeared.

Around that time I started seeing clients at home. I had just retired from the mental hospital where I'd worked as a psychotherapist for over thirty-five years and thought it might be diverting to see the occasional client privately; people with everyday neuroses, shall we say, rather than the psychotics and the severely mentally damaged I had hitherto specialised in.

Antony, my first client, was in his early forties. His presenting problem was insomnia; the reality turned out to be his inability to handle a slowly disintegrating marriage.

Within half an hour Antony revealed his wife had begun to drink heavily (again) and he was certain she was having affairs – with his friends, his colleagues and, possibly, even strangers. She had stayed away several nights, too, claiming to be with girlfriends or her mother.

Antony's clandestine detective work had proven her stories to be fictions. The depth of his jealousy was matched only by worry for his three children, two boys and a girl, all under twelve.

'She neglects them. And I'm out at work all day, earning just enough to pay the mortgage and live,' he complained bitterly, holding back the pent emotion, his face distorting as he fought back the tears.

We agreed weekly sessions and re-evaluation after three months. Thus Antony became a regular, once a week visitor.

Looking back, I like to think I helped him to at least come to terms with himself and his situation, which certainly deteriorated over the months. His wife's drinking became heavier; arguments became fiercer; her affairs became not only more frequent, but more flagrant, until she stopped denying them altogether. He reported all this with the pride of the consummate victim. One night, he had arrived home from work late to find the kids still in school uniform, unfed, watching TV and his wife upstairs, in bed with a total stranger.

'She was laughing at me,' he growled, 'Calling me spineless; saying if I was a real man, I'd have kicked the guy out, beaten him up...'

'Did you want to?' I asked, perhaps cocking my head a little too accusingly and emphasising the word 'want' a tad too much. Psychotherapy is as much technique as intuition.

'No. Yes. I dunno... No, of course not. Not his fault, most blokes would...' he trailed off and in the silence, I observed my irritation rising, recognising my own need to always 'be nice', to avoid confrontation at all costs.

The truth is, three months into our association, I too was finding him frustrating, at times infuriating and, er... spineless. He felt like an encased coiled spring. If only he would acknowledge to himself he was bloody *furious*... How's that for transference?

Eventually, though, Antony began to accept his situation and, more importantly, his own contribution to it; how perhaps his obsessive possessiveness had stifled his wife's yearning for personal growth; that he had rarely communicated his thoughts and feelings; that though they shared a house, a bed, finances and children, he never shared himself. Then she told him she hated him, couldn't stand him near her, or bear his touch.

'You're so weak, so wishy-washy. I fucking *hate* you,' she had screamed at him .

'And, do you know, it didn't touch me. I realised she couldn't hurt me any more,' he crowed. His insouciance, reflecting my own, left me groaning inside.

'And how does that make you feel?' I asked mechanically, technique substituting poorly for inspiration, again, at this juncture.

'That it really is the end of the marriage, I suppose.' He rarely answered that question with actual descriptions of feelings.

So they began to discuss divorce, Antony still trying to be so annoyingly, meticulously fair.

'I'll move out. She can have the house and I'll pay maintenance; all I want in return is to see my kids regularly.'

'And that's all you want?'

'Uh-huh.'

Finally, the dénouement. She ran away with her divorce lawyer (oh! the irony), leaving Antony with the children. He had to give up work and become a full time house husband, something he actually began to enjoy. And still he kept coming to see me, week in, week out.

One day, maybe a year after we'd started, he arrived at the appointed time. It was a beautiful, warm summer's day and we moved our chairs over to the open French windows.

'So, how have you been?' I began, my usual opening.

'Pretty good, actually. And I've got a new girlfriend,' he beamed, a look of total self-satisfaction playing on his face.

'Well, congratulations,' I responded, genuinely pleased for him. 'Where did you meet?'

'I was invited to some friends for dinner. They'd kinda fixed it up and we just clicked. It was magic, really.'

'And what's her name?' I asked. Such questions keep me congruent with my client; showing an interest in what interests them.

'Pandora,' he answered.

At that precise moment, I caught sight of a movement on top of the garden fence to my right. Then a grey flash as a cat dropped down and came strolling, completely unhurriedly, across the lawn towards the open French windows where we sat.

I was somewhat taken aback. It was our old cat, Pandora.

She brushed past my legs and walked straight through my office, making her way to the kitchen where her food bowl used to reside as though the day before was the last time she'd done this instead of over a year prior.

'Antony. You'll have to excuse me for a minute. Something extraordinary has just happened.'

I fed Pandora some tinned tuna – all we had in the fridge and, after

I had explained what had happened to Antony (he didn't share my amazement) and we'd come to the end of our fifty-minute hour, I said goodbye and showed him to the door.

When I returned to write up my notes, Pandora came and snuggled onto one of the easy chairs in my office and fell asleep, exactly as she had spent every afternoon since a kitten, right up to the day she disappeared.

The next morning, she was gone and we never saw her again. And soon after, Antony decided he'd finished with therapy. He and Pandora were to be married; she doted on his children, they adored her, she loved him and he idolised her – and he was happy again.

'I'm cured, Doc. Thanks for everything,' he told me over the phone.

For many years after I asked myself, what are the probabilities of that coincidence happening? How did all those pieces fall into place at that moment? Why did we call our cat Pandora some ten years earlier? Why had Antony's future in-laws chosen the same name for their newly-born and no doubt cherished daughter? What brought us all into contact? Why did our cat decide to return to her birthplace that very day? And what about the timing? Jumping down from the fence at precisely the moment Antony announced the shared name of his new girlfriend?

The mathematics of this all coming so perfectly together are on such vast and incomprehensibly impossible scale, – seemingly programmed into the Big Bang – and yet they did as, somehow, the fabric of space-time warped and momentarily overlapped. Or was it mere chance and the fact that because the possible number of universal events is infinite, duplication is inevitable? That events will, at some point, co-incide? Just as an infinite number of monkeys tapping away on an infinite number of typewriters will, inevitably, produce the complete works of Shakespeare, or so I'm told. I realise that Pandora is not that an usual name, and yet... and yet...

I, of course, have no idea about these things, but Carl Jung, my mentor, wrote about Synchronicity – a word he coined. He claimed that the bigger the coincidence and the more outrageous, the more meaningful it is – all part of the wealth of evidence for a collective unconscious.

Nowadays, an old, old man, sitting and musing, fast approaching the end of my life, I begin to wonder if it tells me, in fact, that we *are* all one; tiny parts of a Creator God, thrust up into a sea of illusion and for-

getfulness. That we are like islands, separate on the surface, yet connected by an ocean floor of hidden reality and that we awaken to the reality
of this only when we die, as Hindus believe.

If that is the truth, are we given gentle half-reminders of this fact;
kept on our toes so to speak by fleeting glimpses of the numinous in our
chance meetings, our dreams, our coincidences?

I can't be certain, of course, the concept has hardly been axiomatic
throughout my life, and yet now, for most of the day, the moment of the
two Pandoras lives as potently alive inside as if I had, for the briefest of
moments, seen into our Creator's mind...

27
THE JOURNEY

SILENCE. NOTHING. THEN a gentle whisper…
'Can you sense our presence?'
No response.
'Are you aware of us now?'
A pause… then acknowledgement.
'Can you understand us?'
'Yes. Yes, I can.'
'Do you know where you are?'
'No… disoriented.'
'You're home.'
'Home?'
'You've been on a journey. Try to remember.'
'Ah, yes, a journey. But so much… all jumbled.'
'What can you recall for us?'
'Uh… nothing – the densest nothing imaginable, then an explosive urge – huge… unbelievable energy, then dazzling light, chaos… outward motion and space-time unfolding. Plus and minus, particles cancelling, coalescing, one in a billion forming, crystallising… Then mass, gravity, density, atoms, elements, molecules... And form, galaxies, stars, planets, all whirling, circling around... Then finally, balance… order.'
'And after?'
'Life – myriad forms, developing, evolving… interaction – mating, breeding, predating; and then the miracle of self-awareness! Civilisations, society… culture… And opposites; always opposites – negative and positive, light and dark, male and female... Power, politics, greed, money, ownership – everywhere, no matter what the sentient species. Wait, there's a scene unfolding:

"I'm afraid we can do no more for you, Sir Henry. The cancer is metastasising."

"How long have I got?"

"Three months perhaps…"

"Huh! I've spent a fortune on treatments to no avail then?"

"I'm sorry. Luckily, you are in a position to buy the best palliative care

available. We'll set up a team of specialist nurses around the clock and..."

"How long will I be compos mentis? Handing over the reins of a multinational is not a simple matter. The board, lawyers, the family... I'll need my wits about me."

"You'll have to balance all that against the pain management regime, Sir Henry."

"The irony. The tenth richest man in the world and I can do nothing to avoid a horrible death..."

'The memory fades now...'

'How did it feel to be that individual?'

'Good. I enjoyed gathering wealth, succeeding, outsmarting others.'

'Do you remember the death?'

'No. Yes! Suddenly slipping away, waking as a child on another planet, with past memory traces. Connections, always interconnectedness, time and space warping...'

'Anything else?'

'Yes. I remember a forest. Covering half a planet, growing towards the light as one. We absorbed our energy from the sun, we sighed in wind and rain, our roots delved into the rich earth, our branches stretching for the sky. And the rhythm of the seasons – we shed our crowns, lay dormant and when our sap rose, produced buds and fresh, new growth. We sheltered and cared for thousands of creatures. It was good. One long inward breath throughout the day – exhaling through the night while we told our stories – the joy of it, the togetherness, the harmony. But then another, more developed species destroyed us, cut us down for fuel and building material.'

'What emotions did you experience?'

'Anger. Sadness... Then acceptance... of playing our part; of returning to pure energy.'

'What next?'

'A queen – I was queen of a vast hive, producing eggs... served by drones – protectiveness, responsibility. Then, I was a high-born male on a planet called Arxus... I was strong, a warrior skilled in fighting. I defended my own ferociously and attacked and killed other men and took their wives and enslaved their children. I fought wars, we conquered and raped and looted and plundered. I revelled in victory, gave no quarter to the vanquished... Yes, yes... remember now – I was killed, in battle.'

'How did that feel?'

'Agonising pain. Horrible... Defeat and hatred. I experienced hatred of my enemies...'

'Tell us more.'

'I remember being female again. Carrying a foetus in my womb. Oh, the joy of creating another being and of giving birth, despite the travail. And the love I felt for my baby... Beautiful... No, oh no, no...'

'What is it?'

'The horror of losing a child – I experienced that, too. I can feel the sorrow – deep, deep sorrow; grief and despair...'

'What else can you tell us?'

'I remember being a great artist and the joy of searching, finding, working, tuning in to creative forces. And being a musician, too – then everything was music and rhythm and texture of sound. I was a scientist, a mathematician, cracking the codes of the fabric of the universe. And a slave – a labourer toiling in fields and down the deepest mines, sweating, muscles aching... I was many a priest, as well, both saint and charlatan – and a Shaman, and a showman... a Pope, too. And a poet, a magician, an addict, a madman... I've also been a thief, a murderer and a paedophile. I've lived on numerous planets in many, many life forms – carbon based, hydrogen based, even lead... I've lived so many lives as microbe, insect, bird of prey, animal, herbivore and carnivore – and as a member of the most technologically developed race... everything and everyone... All coming back to me now. It was glorious, glorious!'

'It has been another remarkable voyage.'

'It has, it has. I've sailed vast seas of methane on gas giants, running before mighty winds; plumbed the depths of oceans, circumnavigated galaxies, dived into black holes, seen stars born and die, climbed mountains, explored caves; and I've wooed and won and been abandoned by lovers; I've danced and laughed and cried and lived... I've seen great civilisations rise and fall, species come and go. I've experienced the dark and the light, the good and evil. I've seen horrors, experienced terror, but above all, love. So much love...'

'And what is your overall impression of this creation?'

'It's good, very good.'

'We'll leave you now, to rest.'

'Rest?'

'You usually need time to reintegrate, to come back to being the selfhood you abandon in order to travel.'

'You mean I've done this before?'

'Yes. You've journeyed an infinite number of times, through innumerable creations.'

'Yes, of course, of course... I'm still a little confused. And I'm puzzled by something... On this journey, I experienced Nirvana, was enlightened, had epiphanies and mystical experiences galore, ever sensing God's presence everywhere, His hand in everything, but never once come face to face with Him. Why is that?'

'Perhaps because you *are* God...?'

ACKNOWLEDGMENTS

I am deeply indebted to Marius, Dirk, my wife, Rosalyn, my grandson, Aaron, my brother, Phillip and my daughter, Amanda, for reading these stories and giving me constant, encouraging feedback – and for acting as editors, pointing out mistakes and errors and supplying astute observations with subtle, improving suggestions.

Thank you all.

BY THE SAME AUTHOR

SAVING GRACE *+
30 Years in Subud
MONKEY TRAP+
A psycho-spiritual novel
JACK'S FRIENDS
An illustrated children's book
ODDS AND SODS*
Essays, articles and jottings
CHRISTMAS IS ON THE CARDS *
40 years of family Christmas cards

THE BLETCHLEY HANDBOOK
A LAUGH WITHIN A LAUGH
THE GREAT LAUGH FORCE
THE GREAT LIFE FARCE *
4 Books of Subud Humour
co-created with Dirk Campbell

* available from www.lulu.com
+ available from www.amazon.co.uk
the rest available from VIA BOOKS,
marcusbolt@easynet.co.uk